Word's

D M ROBERTS

A Novella

Copyright © 2022 D M Roberts
All rights reserved. This book or any portion thereof
may not be reproduced or used in any manner whatsoever
without the express written permission of the publisher
except for the use of brief quotations in a book review. Please respect the hard work of the Author.

Foreword.

Do Angels Exist?
It's an age old question that many have written about, talked about, and given a great deal of thought to over the years.
Could your path be mapped out from the day you enter this world? We, as people, are presented with choices, always. Go left or go right. Take the elevator or the stairs. Sit or stand. There is rarely ever only one option in our daily lives.
Do we have guardians that influence our choices for a reason?
Are we happy to believe there is a higher power keeping things as balanced as we, as humans, like it to be?
Does that faith comfort us in an already mixed up world?
Brian is about to find out that not all things are a random act.

Acknowledgements

Many thanks to you.
My Angel x

Contents

Foreword

Acknowledgement

1 Word's Out

2 A Narrow Escape

3 The Notepad

4 What's in a Name

5 Financial Recompense

6 Old Friends

7 Moving On

8 Before The Committee

9 Rest Easy

10 Pastures New

11 Right Place, Right Time

12 Solitary Moments

13 Gone Fishing

14 There is Always a Plan

!

Word's Out

Brian picked up the espresso from the counter, he had spent his last handful of change to buy the damn thing so, yes, he was going to split hairs with the waitress about it not reaching the middle of the paper cup. She glared at the shabbily dressed man as he stomped out of the coffee shop.

"Some people are so rude!" She continued to whine at her colleague. The teenager shrugged his shoulders. In his mind, he was thinking that he too, would have complained. No time to argue with the angry female, he had tables to clear if he wanted to get off on time.

Outside, Brian walked carefully down the street trying desperately not to spill the precious liquid. It would be customary to be given a lid, not this day. The woman had briskly told him they were out of that size. He had to dodge various obstacles in his aim to make it to the park on the other side of the street.

He would often sit in this particular park, it was nothing special as parks go but it was quiet. He needed a quiet space today, especially today. The bench was empty as it often was at this time of the afternoon. Placing the cup carefully on the slats he slid off his overcoat and sat down.

That first hit of coffee was wonderful, the hot, strong roasted flavour caressed the inside of his mouth as he took in the brew he had missed so much this past week. He returned the cup to the slat and pulled out the crumpled letter from his jacket pocket. Smoothing it out he thought about the anger he had felt earlier today, the fury that rose inside when he first read the wretched thing, screwing it up into a ball in his rage.

He had lived in that house for all of their married life, he couldn't fathom why she would do this to him now. Had he not given her everything she had asked for? She got the business that they had started together, she got the cars, although why she needed both was beyond him and she got the flat and the holiday home. It wasn't as though they had children! No, he had been more than generous with the woman that had betrayed him and now, well he was not going to take this lying down! He felt a fool that she had talked him into signing these assets over to her, to find out that she and her so-called bestie were having it away and had been for some years right under his nose.

Brian, it seemed, had been hoodwinked by the very person that he had trusted the most and now to add insult to injury she was taking away his home. The letter had mentioned that in his absence the court had awarded the property to Martha as recompense for the cruel and long-suffering treatment she had received throughout their marriage. That was a laugh! First off, he had received no such communication of yet another court hearing, secondly, him! Cruel and malicious! If anything she had been the one that had made his life a misery with her constant demands, weekends away and refusal to even consider starting a family.

The letter was stuffed back into his pocket and there he sat, in truth, he had not needed to read it again as he was blessed with a photographic memory, he merely wanted to remind himself that he had not imagined it. Penniless and now, apparently homeless into the bargain. The phone in his pocket let out a shrill burst of music to bring the man back to the ground.

"Hello?"

"Hey, buddy. How are you? Not seen you in ages, where have you been? I heard about you and Martha, course I did, tragic mate, absolutely tragic."

"Hey, Neil. Yeah, I've been busy. Sorry, I haven't returned your calls, I kept meaning to but you know what it's like?"

"We'll have to get together. When is good for you? Linda, has a girl's night tomorrow if you can make that? Awkward, she's meeting up with Martha and her new friend but I'm staying out of that."

"I'll get back to you mate, I'm outside and it's hard to hear you with the traffic."

The truck coming down the street was getting louder as the 2 men tried to continue the conversation.

"What's that mate?" came the voice on the other end of the line.

"I said I can't hear you, I'll get back to you."

"Hello?"

Brian pressed the end call button and picked up his overcoat mumbling to himself.

"Wants to watch she doesn't turn Linda into the same necrotic witch that she has become." He grumbled bitterly as he turned toward the path.

The woman in the coffee shop dropped the tray of mugs as she watched the large truck plough through the rails that surrounded the park.

"Somebody phone the police." She screamed as she ran to the door staring in disbelief at the pandemonium unfolding in front of her. People were running everywhere as the truck came to a grinding halt against the climbing frame. Dust and pieces of metal flew into the air in a cloud of chaos. The park bench was a crumpled mess against the grill of the mangled truck.

"There was a man, there was a man." She screamed to onlookers. She had watched the irritated man through the large windows of the shop as he had made his way into the park not 10 minutes since.

"Stay back love, we have to wait for the police and fire brigade. Bloody lucky the kids are still in school this time of day, it could have been a tragedy. Did you notice anyone else in there?" The woman thought carefully, her mind still in turmoil. Finally, she spoke.

"No, it was quiet over there, I only noticed him because he'd given me a hard time earlier on. I do hope he's alright, never wish harm on him." The onlooker walked the woman back into the coffee shop.

"No doubt you will come in handy as a witness, sit yourself down love and I'll direct them over here when they have a minute."

The emergency services turned up in full force, jumping vigorously from their cabs and setting about their various tasks. The lead officer came over to the coffee shop as directed by the passer-by.

"Which one of you saw the accident?" He asked in the brisk manner that a man of his standing has.

The woman stood, her legs shaking with the adrenalin that was now coursing around her body.

"Me, I saw it all." She replied, her voice now quiet and trembling.

"Let's take a seat over there where it's not so crowded and you can talk me through what happened." The woman sat in the chair, her hands shaking as she grasped the cup her young assistant handed to her.

"Start from the beginning, Miss. Take your time, I know it's been a shock."

"There was a man. I do hope he is okay. I was so harsh with him and he only wanted a coffee. Did you find him?" She sipped on the hot coffee, drops spilling down her clean white t-shirt as she struggled to steady her grip.

"A man? Was he in the park?"

She nodded, looking at him in earnest for an answer.

"I'm sure if he was in there we will find him. You say you were harsh toward him?"

"He complained that we had given him a half-measure in his drink, we had so I refilled it. I watched him walk over to the park, I could see him sitting on the bench, he looked upset you know. I don't think it was because of the coffee." The woman mumbled to herself, trying to reassure her distressed mind that she hadn't caused his despairing thoughts. God forgive her if this was the last thing on his mind at the time of his probable demise.

Outside, across the road, the emergency services were sifting through the crumpled mess that lay before them. The driver of the truck was, by this time, released from his cab and on the way to the hospital. He was unconscious, his head bleeding profusely.

"Did you find anyone else? A witness said there was a man, early 40's, sitting on the bench."

The man in uniform shook his head.

"A couple was walking over the far end and an elderly gentleman with a dog but they're fine and were well out of the way, Sir."

"The bench?"

"As you can see, still attached to the front of the truck, no sign of blood or a person."

The man stared around the remains of the front cab, safe to say the bench was a write-off so where was the man that had occupied it?

2.

A Narrow Escape

Man, it was bright. Maybe he was in a hospital theatre, they had bright lights. The voices he heard were unfamiliar to him, strange and echoey. They seemed to be arguing about something, he couldn't make out what that was exactly no matter how hard he strained to hear. They came closer, dressed in what looked similar to a toga. One of them held a large book in his hand. He assumed it to be a man, for he honestly did not know at this point.

"Ask him." Came the voice, now clearer than earlier.

"I cannot simply ask him, we would appear foolish. We did not get to the station we hold by being foolish."

"If you do not ask him and we are wrong, well, you know who will have us back down to the start. Is that what you want? Do you remember how tedious that was?"

"Then you ask him, I know what I heard, it is written right here!" The figure slammed his finger down on the page of the open book to emphasise his words.

"I do not agree, we cannot have mistakes."

Brian peered at the 2 figures, he must be dreaming. That's it, I must have hit my head and this is a dream.

"Brian Matthew Felling?" The voice addressed him.

"Yes. Who are you, where am I?"

"Now I want you to pay attention to me, Brian. You were making a phone call in the park?"

"Yes, an old friend, Neil."

"Can you remember what happened next?"

Brian stared at the endless brightness above him as he thought. He looked down, the 2 pages of the book before him. His mind scanned the pages of names and localities as he thought about the question. His name was there, it jumped out at him as familiar things often did.

"I heard a truck coming. Wait a minute, am I dead?"

"What happened next, Brian? It is most important that you tell us what you said after you finished your phone call."

Brian stared at the 2 figures, what the hell was going on?

"Where am I? Is this a hospital?"

"This is getting us nowhere, he cannot remember. The best thing we can do is send him for processing and leave it at that."

Processing? What the hell!

"Wait, wait. I was mumbling to myself. Is that what you mean?"

"What did you mumble, Brian? Can you recall?"

Brian tried to sit up, he soon realised he wasn't lying on anything. He seemed to be floating mid-air.

"My wife." He continued, his mind now beginning to panic. "My wife, I was talking about my wife. I said, Neil wants to watch that she doesn't turn Linda into the same necrotic witch that she has become. Yes, that was it. Now can somebody please tell me what is going on here?"

The figures looked at the page, both leaning over the book nodding.

"That makes perfect sense, it was noisy. Yes, that explains everything." They agreed. Standing back from Brian they clapped their hands simultaneously, this was followed by a blinding flash then all went black.

~

"Over here, get the medics I think I've found the man." Called the fireman from the side of the pond. The 3 burly men dragged the soaking and unconscious Brian from the water. They checked for vital signs, he had a faint pulse along with a sharp piece of metal protruding from his stomach.

"Careful guys, we don't want to cause any more damage than he already has." The medic urged.

"Let's get him on the stretcher. You, grab that first aid blanket, get it over him before he catches pneumonia into the bargain."

The ambulance tore through the streets as the paramedics worked tirelessly to keep the soaked man stable.

"What have we got? Oh, that looks nasty, still, he's lucky to be with us, damn lucky you found him from what I hear." The hospital staff transferred Brian onto a bed and he was wheeled straight into the theatre. The operation was a lengthy one, finally, the surgeon, happy with his work, directed that the man could now be stitched up.

Brian lay in his hospital bed for almost 3 weeks before he regained consciousness. When he opened his eyes he panicked. What was in his throat? He couldn't breathe.

"Mr Felling? Try to relax, please don't pull that. Brian? Can you hear me, Brian?" The beeping of the machines told Brian that he was in a hospital. Within seconds the sound of the truck coupled with the memory of the force at which he flew through the air came to him. The other thing must have been a dream, he stopped struggling, letting the wave of relief wash over his mind and body.

"Your wife is outside, do you want me to call her in?"

Brian shook his head carefully. It was pounding making the slightest movements painful.

"You sure now? She's been here every day."

I bet she has, he thought, likely see what else she can get out of me. He nodded slowly. He was sure.

"Okay, it's your decision. You change your mind, you give me a shout, or press the button right here. Try to get some rest now and the doctor will be back to see you within the hour."

He smiled a weak smile. Closing his eyes he could not get the dream out of his head. Over and over the pages flashed in his mind. He needed paper and a pen. Not yet, for now, he needed sleep.

Martha was kept waiting for days after Brian had come around. He had instructed that she was to be told nothing as they were in the process of divorce. Once he had explained the circumstances to the nurses, they were happy to comply with his request. They felt sorry for the man, he had lost everything to the cool, collected woman that sat in the waiting room day after day.

It was Wednesday morning, the nurse had finished helping Brian to do his morning exercises and bathroom needs. She took the bag of laundry from the room and headed off down the corridor.

The door opened quietly.

"I knew it!" Shouted Martha, standing there with hands on hips staring at Brian.

"What do you want? I have nothing left to give you if that's why you're here."

"Don't be so melodramatic Brian, it doesn't suit you. In case you forgot, we were married a long time. I simply wanted to make sure that you were alright, is that a crime?"

Brian shrugged, it ached to do so but the body has its inbuilt habits.

"We have been discussing the matter, Jayne and I. We have decided that you may rent the house for the time being, at a reasonable rate of course. It simply would not do to have you staying on a friends couch in your current condition. I think it's very generous of us, considering."

He almost laughed, he couldn't it hurt too much. Was this woman for real? Martha continued.

"I imagine it will take you some time to get back on your feet. I can wait, it's not like we need the money. Well, that's all I came to say really, I do hope you are up and about soon. You have my number if you need anything. Take care." She was gone, like the snake in the grass that slithered in, she slithered out. Mighty big of her and Jayne! He would have the last laugh, he didn't know how or when but he would.

Brian picked up the notepad and pen, the nurse had kindly found one for him and over the past few days, he had begun to write down the list. It was too vivid for him to simply shake off, he knew there was something more to it than a dream. The areas were spread far and wide and the names were evidently from people of different countries. It was the random words next to each name that he could not figure out. What did it all mean? Next to his name was the word neurotic, he didn't dare utter the word, not after the conversation of the 2 figures played in his head like a reel on a loop. They had argued about something he had said, that he knew for sure. Was he going crazy? It had been a hell of a year, stress can do strange things to a person. The back page of the notepad had questions, to some it would look like the rantings of a deranged man. These questions needed answers, trouble was, where would he get these answers? He placed the pad to one side, he was tired.

3.

The Notepad

It was Friday morning, 2 weeks later that Brian was wheeled down to the waiting cab. He could walk, the nurse had insisted that he take the wheelchair until he was through the door. Hospital procedure, she grinned.

"You are quite sure there's no one you want me to call to collect you?" She asked in the room.

"No, that's very kind of you. I have no-one is the truth."

"Oh, before you leave. Somebody left this for you, I don't know who it was before I came on shift." She handed him an envelope as he took his first breath of outside air in a long-time.

"You take care Brian, don't forget what we talked about. You have to keep up with those exercises."

Brian waved back, she had been a wonderful nurse, he had grown fond of the happy-go-lucky woman. The driver opened the door, helping Brian into the cab from the chair.

"Where to?"

Brian recited his address to the man, they pulled away from the hospital grounds heading for home.

Martha had insisted on picking him up to which he had refused, instead, she left an envelope of bills to cover the cab fare. Brian did not refuse this, he wasn't going to pay it back either! That was for damn certain.

The house felt cold and dark with a musty smell in the air. It smelt as a house would when there has not been a body living in it. Brian closed the door to the noisy street outside. Now he could concentrate on the matter that would not leave his mind alone. It was only when he sat down in the comfortable chair that had been his favourite for many years that he remembered the note in his pocket. It was from the woman in the coffee shop, she wished him well and that his recovery was a speedy one, she went on to write of how sorry she felt that she had been so hard on him the morning of the accident. She hoped that when he was feeling better he would call by, coffee on the house, that she could apologise in person. Well, that was nice of her he thought. If he was feeling up to it he might just take a walk over there tomorrow.

The mail had stacked up over the weeks he had been in the hospital, he stared at the stack of unopened envelopes on the table. No time like the present. There were the usual bills, mostly with red ink, some junk mail and various correspondence from his business. He paused, not his business anymore, these he tossed to one side. There were 2 letters from his solicitor, one regarding the house, the other regarding a claim for compensation from the truck company and his insurance.

"Now we're talking." He said out loud. According to his solicitor, there could be the potential of a lot of money coming his way. The company had admitted liability after extensive reports from witnesses and the emergency services, all Brian had to do was submit the claim. Was it that easy? Most companies would drag these sorts of things through the courts for years and yet here was one that was willing to get the whole sorry incident sewn up as soon as they could. It was true to say they were a well-known and large household name, he imagined it would not be in their interest to have this go even more public than it had so far. Yes, he would submit the claim, he could have been killed!

After a light, easily prepared dinner, Brian lay on the couch. Pushing the remote on his music system he lay quietly as the soft orchestral music floated through the air. It wasn't long before he fell into a deep sleep.

~

"Do you think he knows?"

The figure shrugged.

"He is making a lot of lists, but he could not, it is not possible. Is it?"

"You of all beings should know that anything is possible. What should we do?"

"We should watch him, carefully. If there is the smallest chance that he does know, well, we shall simply have to intervene."

"How? We have never had to intervene in the past."

"We have never before faced such an issue. Although, there was, or rather is, that man in India. Maybe this one will be content to simply, you know, live his life."

The figure shook his head, he had a funny feeling about this one.

"I am not convinced. I think perhaps it is best that we nip this in the bud."

"You mean own up to, Him? He will not be happy, you realise this?"

Again the figure stared at his companion with an awkward gaze. This was a mess, what's more, they had created it.

"We shall see. Come along the time is ticking and we still have other duties to carry out. We can come back to this."

Opening his eyes, he could swear he heard voices. They had a familiar pitch to them that he couldn't quite place. Time for bed. He clicked off the music centre and carefully pulled the blinds before he headed off to bed clutching his notepad. Coming out of the bathroom he looked around the room that had once been full of expensive furniture, now it contained a standard bed and a dresser. She had even taken the bedside tables and lamps, still, it was warm and comfortable.

He propped himself up against the pillows, he loved his pillows.

Martha had always complained that he had far too many on the bed making it impossible for her to get a good night sleep without being accosted by the mountain of cushions every time she turned over. Now at least, he could have as many as he wanted.

Brian flicked through the names, a few he recognised from the papers and T.V. Only a few mind you. The others were as unrecognisable to him as the pages in the phone book. The pattern was emerging in the list as he read them over and again. Some names were closely situated to others geographically. Did this mean something?

He began rewriting them, this time he grouped them by locality. What did it all mean? He closed his eyes as he replayed the dream he thought he had experienced on the day of the accident. The voices came to him like a flash of lightning, that's where he had heard them! The same sounds he heard earlier as he lay dozing. Was there someone in the house maybe? Don't be ridiculous, he told himself.

They were arguing about what he had said, wanted him to be exact in his wording when they questioned him, very insistent on that as he could recall. Then what? He repeated what he had said and woke in the hospital. He began scribbling his crazy sounding thoughts frantically until he eventually laid the pencil down. Reading what he had written he laughed to himself.

"They will lock you up for sure." He howled into the quiet night.

He would do some more investigating tomorrow, it had been a long day and he was tired, his injury was throbbing as he lay down and pulled the covers over himself.

"Listen, pal, you've had a serious accident, not to mention barely escaping death so it's natural you will have weird dreams and thoughts. Do you want to talk about them?"

Brian did not, not in detail at any rate.

"No, if you think it's normal I'll go with that. Just forget I mentioned it. Sorry, I never made that drink the other week."

Neil laughed, he was a funny man.

"I hardly think what happened to you was your way of getting out of a drink with me. Loosen up man, we are having a drink now aren't we? So, Linda met the new partner. Not a fan, I have to say."

"No? Any reason?"

Neil gulped down on his beer, his grin causing the alcohol to drip down his chin.

"Too pushy she said, asking too many questions. You know my Linda, she's the private sort. She said it was what she imagined being grilled in the witness box must be like."

Brian relaxed a little, this made him snigger. He knew Linda from old and she wasn't the kind of woman that took to being interrogated.

"Did she have to swear on the bible before she gave her answers?" The 2 men roared at the comment.

"Oh, hell that hurts." Holding his side, Brian grimaced as the pain seared across his stomach.

"Note to self, do not make the stiff laugh."

"Less of the stiff if you don't mind. Speaking of which, I have a solicitor coming by tomorrow to go over the claim. They are not going to contest it, so I should have a bank balance that will finally be back to being in the black for the first time since the separation. I'm tempted to put it into a different one, what do you think?"

Neil put his serious face on, he knew far too well the cost of divorce.

"Tell her nothing, get it in an off-shore account. My lips are sealed, plus she has taken everything you had, this is yours."

It was strange to be sitting here, like old times without the wives. They had been friends a long time and Brian was well aware that he had let things slide since the separation and subsequent divorce. He naturally assumed that Linda and Martha had a strong bond and thus, there would be no room in their small circle for him. It was good to hear that Linda was not impressed with his stand-in, he couldn't abide awkward situations and there was bound to be many to come. Linda and Neil had children that were growing up fast, there would be weddings, christenings, and such like in the not so distant future. Yes, this news suited him wonderfully.

"Do you want me to come round to your place as a witness when the stiff comes?" Neil interrupted his musings.

"If you're not busy, he's coming over around 11, I would be grateful for your thoughts."

"No problem pal, I'll drop the rug rats off at school and come straight there. Can't wait for Tyrone to get his car back, I feel like the oldest parent when I look at the Mom's congregating around the drop-off point. They get younger, I swear they do."

"None take your fancy?" laughed Brian.

"It's not that they don't, I wouldn't have the energy! My Linda makes sure of that." The 2 men carried on talking and drinking for a good while until Neil caught the time on his watch.

"Got to go buddy, you're sure you won't come by for something to eat? We're having Mexican."

"Thanks for the offer, I doubt my stomach could withstand the onslaught of your spices just yet. See you tomorrow?"

"You sure will, adios amigo." He waved behind his head as he left the bar. Brian finished his drink and he too headed outside. The sun was beginning to set, it looked beautiful in all its glorious orange colours.

4.

What's In a Name

~

The house was warmer than it had been of late, the day had been a hot one that had aided the alcohol in Brian's system. He had not looked at the notepad once today. He meant to try and put things together, somehow the invitation from Neil seemed far more appealing. He began the descent up to bed. From behind the door, he could hear that sound again, he stopped, his ear getting closer to the wood as he tried to hear what was being said in his bedroom. The voices, as there were 2 of them, were talking about his notepad.

"We cannot take it, you know as well as I that we cannot transfer items to the beyond. There is also the matter that he would simply write it out again. Have you considered that?"

"Can we not erase his memory? Surely that is permissible under the circumstances?"

"Ludicrous idea, we cannot intervene in this way. Why it goes against all of our values."

"Difficult times call for difficult measures, do you not agree?"

"Not in this case. We have a duty to uphold His rules."

"I am not denying this, still, if it all comes down around our ears, He, will want to know why."

Brian pushed the door open slowly, through the crack he could see the 2 figures clearly. He rubbed his eyes, it was so bright in there. He must be dreaming, what had he been drinking? If he didn't know any better he would swear he could see 2 Angels standing next to his bed. The door creaked as he lost his grip on the handle.

The figures turned toward him, their faces shrouded in the bright light that encased their frames.

"We did not hear you return, come in Brian."

Walking slowly into the room, Brian could not take his eyes off the pair.

"Sit, please. We have a bit of a situation here, do we not?"

The man sat on the edge of the bed.

"Who are you?" That was all he could manage to say.

"We are, well I suppose you would refer to us as Angels here on Earth. Celestial Beings as such."

"But you can't be, I'm dreaming, I must be dreaming. Yes, that's it, in a minute I'm going to wake up and you won't be here."

"Ah, but we will. We are real Brian. Tell me, do you believe, Brian?"

"Believe in what?"

The 2 figures glanced at each other. Surely he could grasp what they were talking about. They knew that many on the planet had lost their faith but everyone knew what the question meant?

"In Him, Brian. Do you believe in Him?" The figure pointed upward.

"God? You're talking about God, right?"

"If that is how you refer to Him, then yes, God. Do you believe in God, Brian?"

Brian ran his fingers through his hair, this was not happening. Wake up, wake up now!

"Well do you, Brian?"

"Of course I do, who doesn't? I mean, some say they don't and that's fine, they still call out for him so they must still think he's there, I guess."

"Good answer. Then you believe in Celestial Being's, they go hand in hand don't they?"

"I suppose so, I don't think I've given it that much thought. What do you want with me?"

"You witnessed a mistake, Brian. Our fault entirely, it has to be said, a mistake, nonetheless. Why are you so insistent on going over the pages that you saw? We know you saw them, we know you committed them to memory. It will only lead to trouble if you continue to pursue it."

"I need to know what it means."

"You do not. It is no concern of yours." Replied the second figure, he had remained quiet for the most part.

"I can't unsee it, that's the truth of it." Brian clasped his hands together as he stared down at the floor.

"But you must. These things are bigger than you, bigger than us. They are part of a carefully laid plan and you must not interfere."

"What plan? He has no plan. You only have to look around to see that. Once, maybe, not now."

"You are quite wrong. There is always a plan, it may not be to everyone's liking but there is always a plan, Brian."

Brian shook his head. Where was this great plan when his wife left him? No, where was the plan when his parents were killed? Nowhere, that's where.

"Will you agree to leave this alone, Brian?"

"There is nothing to leave alone, I wasn't going to do anything with it, who would believe me anyway?"

"Quite right, they would think you mad. Look at the great Son, what happened there is a lesson to you. People do not want to hear what you have to say." The second figure was getting annoyed with the man, he had no right to poke his nose into matters that were beyond his fathoming.

"We can trust you with this?"

Brian nodded, he knew in his mind that he wasn't going to leave it there but they did not.

"Yes, think no more of it."

~

Darkness descended on the room, they had gone leaving Brian alone with his thoughts. He switched on the television as he settled back against the pillows. The tail end of the local news was wrapping up. The newscaster was talking about a freak accident in Montana.

"Mr Lance Prendergast was a well-liked member of the Livingston community and close friends say they are shocked at the news of his sudden death."

Why was that name familiar? He must have heard it earlier in the bar, perhaps. Time was marching on, if he had any hope of getting himself up in the morning he must switch off the T.V and get some sleep. Dragging himself to the bathroom his mind turned to his friend, Neil. It irked him that he had ignored the man for so long, it wasn't in his nature that was for sure. Brushing his teeth he stopped suddenly as the names flashed in his head.

"Bloody hell." His voice rang out in the quiet house. Throwing the brush into the sink he ran into the bedroom, picked up the notepad and scanned it. There it was, as clear as day! How had he not known this? On the page he had written, ***Lance Prendergast – Livingston, Montana – DEBACLE***

"Bloody hell, Oh Lord!" Brian began to panic, he sat on the edge of the bed staring at the page.

There was another name from the same area, what should he do now? Could he warn them? What would he be warning them against, he wasn't quite sure but he knew he had to do something. The town was Polson, also in Montana, the name quite obviously a woman. He grabbed the phone directory from the floor then tossed it back down, that would be of no use as he wasn't even in the same state.

"Well, there's nothing I can do tonight." Resigning himself to that fact he climbed into bed once more for a restless night's sleep.

~

"He is not going to leave it alone, you know that as well as I do. We have to do something, we have this course of action in place for a reason. You know I am right?"

The figure paced back and forth, he had to think.

"Are you listening to me? I said we have to do something."

"Yes, yes I am well aware of that. Be quiet whilst I think."

"We are wasting far too much time on this human, this should have been dealt with at the time of the incident."

"If you had not misheard we would not be in this mess."

"I hardly think that this is the time for blame. We need to deal with this as soon as we can."

5.

Financial Recompense

They made their way into the hall, there were many beings of the same dress gathered there as they took their place at the back, still whispering to each other. It was a bright hall that appeared to have no walls, ceiling, or floor. To an outsider, it would appear they were suspended in mid-air. The room fell quiet as a smaller being entered. They were not called to the great room often, only in exceptional circumstances.

The quiet was deafening as the beings waited for the figure to speak.

"It would seem we have a glitch. It is not unheard of, I grant you that, there have been 1 or 2 over the millenniums. Our focus now would be to rectify this glitch. The Almighty hears all, he sees all. It would serve you well to remember this when your time comes for your interview. I should stress that this is a very serious matter, should any here amongst us wish to come forward I urge you to do so now, rather than later." His voice did not match his stature, it boomed out across the room causing the gowns that they wore to vibrate.

"They know!" Hissed the figure.

"Not possible, we have been careful."

"Did one of you want to say something?" Came the booming voice.

The figures went quiet again.

"I shall wait here should any of you wish to come to me privately. Think about it carefully."

The room began to empty amid whispering from the hordes of beings that had occupied it.

"What do we do?"

"We do nothing. It could be that it's nothing to do with our dilemma, to offer ourselves up without knowing this would be folly."

"Azrael, you understand the consequences if we are found out? They will be dire."

"I understand fully, Dumah. I feel we need to give this being time to prove himself."

The voice interrupted their whispering.

"Dumah, Azrael, you have a mind to speak with me?"

"No, St Peter, we have no mind to speak with you regarding the matter."

"As you wish." The small figure walked away, his head shaking as he did so.

"Now you have done it! You have sealed our fate without so much as a consultation." Dumah hissed as he pushed past the figure.

~

Brian woke early that next morning, he showered and changed his dressing then headed downstairs. His home was lacking in niceties, he knew this. Since the divorce, Martha had slowly but surely stripped it of furniture and pictures. He began tidying away newspapers and coffee mugs before the arrival of the solicitor. There, that was marginally better, he thought as he sat at the breakfast bar. He ate a breakfast of muesli and fruit as he had done for many years. The smell of the coffee reminded him that he must make an effort to go into the coffee shop and thank the waitress for her kind note.

He had barely finished washing the dishes up when the bell rang. It was earlier than expected, at least half an hour to be precise.

"Morning buddy, you did remember that I was popping around?" Said Neil as he stepped into the hallway. Of course, they had arranged it the day before.

"Come in, help yourself to coffee. It's just made, he should be here in 30 minutes or so."

Neil whistled as he walked through to the kitchen.

"She sure did a number on you! I didn't realise that she had left you with so little. Linda mentioned that she had taken a few personal belongings but this! This is more like a burglary. Why did you give it over so easily buddy?"

Brian shook his head, Neil hadn't been around since the split and had seen the house fuller in previous years than it was now.

"Seemed easier at the time, coupled with the fact that she had me believe it was down to me. It's only things pal, things that we none of us need."

"It's a disgrace and now I hear she wants your house."

"She has the house, it was decided by the time I received the letter to inform me."

Neil was speechless, he sat at the breakfast bar nursing his coffee mug.

"Take it back to the courts! You can tell them that in light of the new information regarding her adultery you want it looked at again."

"I couldn't afford to is the truth, she's cleared out the bank accounts and has full ownership of the company that I built, I don't have a leg to stand on if you look at it on paper. We had the company transferred to her name years ago as a tax dodge of sorts, her idea, naturally. Tell me, Neil, am I so gullible?"

Neil stared at his friend, what could he say?

"You trusted your wife of 22 years buddy, that's not gullible, that's marriage."

The solicitor arrived bang on 11, he was younger than they expected but then everyone was getting younger in their professions these days, or maybe they were simply getting older.

"Good morning Mr Felling. So good to see you up and about. Shocking what happened but you look well. Shall we get down to it?"

"Thank you, good morning. This is my Neil, I thought it a good idea to have him here in case I miss anything you say."

"Not an issue, in fact, we recommend it. Now, I have spoken at length with the Bradigan company legal team and they are willing to make you an offer. It does not, however, mean that you are obliged to accept it. We tend to disregard the first offer in cases such as this, although I will say, it is quite a substantial one. After going over the emergency services reports they know without a doubt that they will never win this in court, plus, they have a reputation to uphold. Here is the offer they have put forward, now, this also covers any long term problems that may show themselves in the long term, health-wise. They have already paid the hospital costs which is good form on their part. We usually have to drag companies kicking and screaming to get this initial cost out of the way. I would say that you are a very fortunate man to have been involved with this particular firm Mr Felling." He coughed with embarrassment at his last statement.

"That is to say, had you been injured by certain other parties the outcome may not have been as plain sailing as this."

Brian smiled, he had understood what the man was getting at.

"Do you think they have offered a fair settlement?" Neil asked.

"Take a look for yourself." The solicitor pushed the piece of paper toward Neil.

"CHRIST!" was Neil's shocked reply.

Brian daren't look, if Neil's reaction was anything to go by it was either a pittance or a fortune.

"You were expecting more?" Inquired the suited young man.

"No, no, not at all. It's a bloody king's ransom, Brian. Look!"

Brian pulled the paper nervously toward him as the man continued.

"As I said, we don't have to accept this, mighty generous in my mind, but you did suffer an enormous trauma."

Brian looked down at the figure, he could feel his heart beginning to race, beads of sweat began forming on his brow as he struggled to comprehend what he was reading.

6.

Old Friends

~

Azrael did not make his presence known, but simply stood, as he often did, watching the old man. The heat was a dusty one as often was the case in this part of the world. The old man waved to his Great-grandchildren he was waving to the sky, to him he was waving to an old friend. The Great-grandchildren said nothing, for that was his way. He was a very old man and should the want be there for him to wave at the sky, who were they to tell him differently?

Azrael waved back as was his way. He had been coming here for nigh on a century to watch the man. He looked strangely older today, true he was aged beyond human comprehension yet today he looked it. The Great-grandchildren got back to their work. The old man, now sitting alone, crooked his finger toward the sky. This was new, thought the figure. He stood beside the old man.

"Hello, old friend."

"Blessings to you. You have need to speak with me?"

The old man shuffled on the ground, his body ached, his mind ached.

"I am tired, old friend, I grow weary of this changing world."

Azrael smiled down to the man, a soft smile that placed a feeling of peace into the old man's heart.

"Would you like to leave now?" He asked quietly.

"I would. I have done all that I am going to do here."

Azrael leant beside the old man, his face close as he whispered in his ear. The old man chuckled, nodded his head, and stared back at the figure.

"How did I miss that, you are a sneaky one old friend."

"We do what we must dear one."

"We have seen some things in our time together. I shall miss your quiet company."

"As I shall miss yours. Are we ready?"

"It is time, let the Almighty take me into his home and death be my new beginning."

The old man closed his eyes for the last time in the heat of the Indian sun, his hand losing its grip on Azrael's as he slipped peacefully to the next journey.

"I thought he would hang on longer than that. Does it make you sad?"

Dumah stood beside his counterpart. He knew well enough the curious friendship the 2 had struck up.

"I thought it would make me happy, after all, in the beginning, he found the loophole and no matter what was tried he beat it every time. Now, I see him for the man he was and that man was a good man. He did wondrous things with his stolen time. Does it make me sad? Yes, it makes me sad that he feared the inevitable for such a long time. There is a reason that they do not know, it saddens me for a life wasted, lived in fear. He will see that now." Azrael stood up from the dusty ground.

"Come, we have work to do."

~

Brian was sitting in the coffee shop, the television on the wall in the corner was switched on, the volume low. It was playing a music channel, he hummed along to the song not remembering the words. The young man at the counter had asked him to wait, she was due on shift he explained, would be in shortly. The coffee was on the house, she had left word that should he call by he was not to be charged. The door swung open, the tinkle of the bell ringing out like a bird song in his ears. Brian watched as the woman made her way behind the counter, apologising for taking so long. It seemed she had car trouble. He looked at her now, for the first time he looked at her properly. She was quite an attractive, girl next door type.

Strange, he hadn't noticed in all the years he had been coming in here. Her mousy tousled hair was being swept up into a messy bun, she tied the apron strings around her slim waist as the young man spoke to her in a hushed voice. She glanced over to his table, smiled, a sweet warm smile that made Brian feel good. How old must she be? He thought as he watched her. 45 perhaps, she wasn't in her twenties although he imagined she could pass for 35. He shook his head and looked away, back to the T.V screen.

The music was no longer playing, a customer had switched the channel, most likely to get game results from the news programme. Brian sat up in his chair, the reporter was talking about one of the oldest men alive. He had passed away peacefully in India. The man had achieved many amazing things in his long lifetime. People would travel clear across the world to visit him, trying to gain the secrets of his seemingly limitless existence. Some reports believed him to have been at least 134 years old, incredible, she continued as the man came so close to death in his 50's.

"Hey, you. I am so pleased to see you are okay. You gave us quite a scare there when the, you know, happened. First off, I feel truly awful about my mood that day. I keep asking myself, if I hadn't been so rude to you would you have sat in the park? Crazy I know, you sit in it often, can't always be because of my attitude, could it?" She pulled out a chair and sat opposite Brian as she continued to talk. She seemed nervous as she rambled on, drowning out the voice on the T.V

"I have no good excuse for the way I spoke to you, I had some news you see. That morning, the day you came in. Not that it's your problem I know, oh, listen to me prattling on like an idiot. How are you?" She sighed, her body relaxing now that she had gotten that out of the way.

"I'm doing okay, thank you for asking. Listen, there is really no need for you to say sorry. I do sit in the park a lot, since I retired from my business, I doubt anything you said contributed to what happened. I'm Brian, by the way."

"Mel, people call me Mel. Nice to meet you, Brian."

"Mel it is. Is that short for anything?"

"Melanie, I haven't been called Melanie since I was a child. You're young to be retired? Oops, not my business, I'm so sorry I am not normally so scattered. I was beginning to worry you see, I called the hospital but you know what it's like, if you aren't a relative they tell you nothing."

Brian nodded, he was intrigued by this woman. She had a way about her that kept his interest, how had he not noticed this in the past? That said, since the divorce, he had barely looked up, before the divorce, well, it just wasn't his way. He had always been a 1 woman man.

They chatted well into the afternoon, he liked her!

It was their first real date, Brian was nervous no matter how much Neil tried to calm him down.

"It will be fine. You haven't told her about the money have you?"

Brian frowned at his overly cautious friend. Was he that bad a catch on his own merit?

"No I haven't, do you think that's the only reason she thinks I'm a catch?"

"No, not at all. You're a handsome, single, walking miracle, my friend. She will be lucky to have you. I'm only looking out for your best interests Brian. The less she knows about that side of things, the better it is for you."

"What if she does know? Do you think it's the reason she's showing interest in me?"

"I doubt it, sure most folks will imagine you must have gotten a payout of some kind, they just won't know you hit the mother load. Unless you tell them"

"Yes, I assume they will think it's a court thing that will drag on forever. There is something really sweet about her. Who knows, if all goes well we may be able to set up a dinner date so you can meet her."

"Who says I haven't already checked her out." Grinned Neil.

"You're such a total tool." barked Linda from the kitchen.

"Well? Will I do?" Brian stood in the kitchen, his best denim jeans and jacket combo. Linda laughed.

"I don't know what possessed that wife of yours to ever look in anyone else's direction, let alone someone of the same sex. That's not fair, same-sex is fine but have a personality for God's sake. She's so dull!"

"Takes all sorts I guess. Times are changing my girl, you're lucky I manage to fight the fella's off at work or things could be very different."

"Fool, the fella's at work have more taste." She laughed as she leant in to kiss her husband.

"Right, best be off. I don't want to make a bad impression on our first date."

The restaurant was crowded. He had been lucky to secure them a booth at such short notice, Neil had helped with that as he knew the owner quite well. Mel arrived moments after Brian, she had insisted on making her own way there. Few things to do on the way, she had said.

The waiter took her to the table, Brian stood up as Mel was seated.

"You look so different." He had noticed this when he saw her enter the room, along with several of the other male occupants. She had a glow about her, maybe the lighting in here, he thought.

"Different good?" She smiled.

"Oh, absolutely. Not that you don't look good on any other day, is what I mean. Different as in well put together. Oh dear, I'm not starting off on a good foot am I?" He laughed nervously. Idiot! He screamed in his head.

"You too look good, very good. I love that jacket. Is it suede?"

"Thank you, yes I've had it for years, it's a favourite of mine. I'm rambling. What would you like to drink?"

"Bourbon on the rocks please, it's been one of those days." Hmm, she liked bourbon.

"Is that okay with you?" She looked embarrassed now as she watched him from across the table.

"Perfectly okay, you don't often hear of women drinking bourbon, took me back is all."

"I limit myself, you'll be pleased to hear." Her laugh was simply beautiful, like a melody that hung in the air.

~

Azrael smiled, this was nice.

"I thought I would find you here. Any news?"

As ever, Dumah was straight to the point.

"It looks promising, he hasn't picked the notepad up in over 2 weeks. I think it may be safe to say he has other things to occupy his mind."

"Have you been called to your meeting yet? I have mine shortly."

"Not yet, I hear there is some debate surrounding a human's entry into the Beyond. You can rest easy that our, situation, is still undiscovered."

Dumah shrugged, he had no qualms about doing the right thing should his hand be forced, Azrael was under no illusions about this.

"Shall we leave the happy pair? We have business in Italy, I do love Italy, the great shame, of course, is that we cannot sample the food. Oh, to have one meal, it would last me a lifetime." Azrael laughed quietly. Honestly, this counterpart would have made a splendid, if not plump, human being.

7.

Moving On

~

"Another bourbon?" Asked Brian as they finished off their meal.

"No, I wouldn't dare. I make it a rule to have 1 a week, that's quite enough for me. A glass of wine will do nicely."

There was something vaguely familiar about what she said, Brian couldn't help thinking he had heard this rule at some other time in his life. No matter, he thought as he pushed it from his mind and ordered more wine. It turned out they had a lot more in common than they first thought. They both came from the area, had gone to school here, both dropped out of college to start up their own business, they were both single recently due to one reason or another. They neither of them had children, a thing they both regretted during their respective marriages but less so on Brian's part since his marriage break-up. Yes, their lives read quite similarly on paper. They talked nonstop during dessert with Mel reminding Brian of the gym teacher in the high school.

"Oh wow, I do remember her! All the boys were mad crazy in love with her. The girls not so much."

"She was a hard act to follow. Always perfectly made up, she never broke a sweat, which I have to say I found quite strange. Shame what happened to her, she was a nice person."

"What happened to her? You lost me there."

Mel lowered her voice as she looked furtively around the room.

"You didn't hear? She was shot by her husband, it was in all the local papers. Must have been about

20 odd years ago now. I can't believe you didn't know. He came home early from work, he worked away a lot by all accounts. Anyway, he comes in and there's a man in the shower right? He does no more than takes his daddy's shotgun from the closet and shoots her where she stands as she comes through the kitchen door. Thinks she's up to no good you see, turns out, and this is the real tragedy of it all, it's her brother in the shower, home on leave unexpectedly." Mel sat back, her breathing fast and loud.

"Jesus! That is a terrible thing. What happened to him? The husband."

"Still in the big house, as far as I know, a crime of passion and an unfortunate case of mistaken identity so the judge said, brother never forgive himself and was killed in active duty, some say he went looking to meet his maker."

"That is some story, what a bad way to go if there is a good way of course."

"Tragic, such a waste of life. Well are we not just the happiest conversationalists ever!" she laughed as she looked at the now stricken expression on her dinner date's face.

Brian walked her to the car, he was unsure what the proper protocol was in this day and age. It had been a long, long time since he had taken a woman out to dinner that hadn't been his wife. Mel stepped forward, kissed him lightly on the cheek and grinned.

"There, that's the awkward moment over with, I know you were thinking about it."

"You know far too much about me. Should I be concerned?" He grinned back.

"Oh, I don't know. Would it concern you to know that I thoroughly enjoyed myself, more than I have in a good while? Or would the concern come if you find me in your kitchen tomorrow morning?" Her face was dead pan as she spoke.

"Are you one of those crazy dames that my mother warned me about?"

"Depends, are you looking for a crazy dame?"

Mel put the key in the door of the pickup truck.

"I like your wheels, not what I expected I have to say."

"This old beast, I just adore it. It's practical, reliable and looks cool. Everything a girl looks for."

"Is that so? Well, right there are some qualities a guy will have to work on to live up to. Do I stand a chance?"

Mel sat in the driver seat, pulling the heavy door shut she put the key in the ignition.

"You have infinite qualities, Brian, I think we can say your chances are like the espresso you love so much." The truck pulled away as Brian called after her.

"What does that mean?"

"Strong Brian, strong."

He watched the lights fade as the truck disappeared into the dark night.

~

Azrael waited patiently for Dumah to come out of the room. To say it felt like an eternity was putting it mildly for he knew what a real eternity felt like. Eventually, the figure appeared.

"And?"

"And, what?"

"Do they know?"

Dumah's face was hard to read, his chiselled features altered not one bit, giving nothing away.

"Stop worrying, they do not know. You will find out soon enough, I dare say it won't help you for me to discuss the actual reason for the meeting, they can tell. All I will say is it does not relate to our present issue."

Azrael sighed his relief. He needed time to sort this one out in his way, only then, would he confess his mistake to the Almighty. The figures disappeared down the bright walkway.

~

Neil sat in the garden, he was impatient to hear about the date.

"Be with you in a sec, do you want a beer?"

"Beer would be good, come on man, I want to hear all the juicy details. I crave excitement and if the only excitement I'm going to get is yours then let's go."

Brian handed the can to his friend. Flipping the burgers over on the grill he groaned.

"I thought you were keeping an eye on these. You're getting the charred one, you know that, right?"

"My bad, I forgot. I'm not the barbecue type of guy, you know that."

"Here, take a look at this. It's the latest offer from that company. Personally, I would have been happy with the initial offer but the solicitor says not. He said it has to make them conscious of their blame or some such BS."

Neil unfolded the letter, his face told the story of surprise as he scanned the words and figures.

"Take it, there's enough money to last you 3 lifetimes if you're sloppy with your finances, take it,

Brian, that's my advice. They could always withdraw if you turn it down, I realise they have a reputation but even these guys will draw the line somewhere."

Brian had to admit his friend had a point, he had no intention of going through a lengthy court process.

"I agree, I am going to tell them to accept the offer. I know this kid wants to make a name for himself, they always do. Not on my case he isn't."

"So, what you going to do with it?" Neil sunk his teeth into the hot juicy burger, it was delicious.

"I haven't given it too much thought. Yes, I know you think that's crazy but I haven't. I feel it's tempting fate in a way, get it in the bank first off and then decide."

"Fair enough. Now to more pressing matters, how did the date go? Did you get on? Did you go back to hers for a little slap and tickle? Come on, spill."

Brian swallowed his mouthful with some difficulty. Was this guy the funniest or what?

"You're terrible buddy, a gentleman never reveals such things. Yes, we got on like a house on fire. The evening went so fast it was over before it had started, in a good way. I like her, you know. She's easy-going, funny, not too hard on the eyes either."

"So, you're seeing her again?"

"I hope so. We didn't set a date or anything."

"Get over there and set one, you don't want her wondering if she's going to hear from you again, that's just cold. Women don't like that, take it from me."

"Oh yeah, last time you had a date?"

"You know what I mean man. I hear my daughter all the time, Oh, do you think he'll call, should I call him, it's been a MONTH! Get over there and put the girl out of her misery. Of course, there is another possibility."

"Which is?"

"She might not want another date, once might have been enough, you hear me?"

Brian threw the remainder of his burger at his friend, picking it up and wiping the dirt from it, Neil stuffed it into his mouth.

"Animal!" Laughed Brian.

8.

Before the Committee

~

Azrael entered the room, he bowed to the committee that sat before him. St Peter occupied the middle space.

"Come forward."

He did as he was instructed.

"Introduce yourself."

Azrael wondered why he had to introduce himself, they knew who he was, more protocol.

"Azrael, Angel of Death, Archangel chief of the Guardian Angels."

"You know why you have been summoned?"

"I do not." He shifted uneasily as he said this.

"We have a matter come to our attention. The human in question has, for most of his life been a fine, upstanding person in his community. However, he has not always been so. It is our responsibility to make a judgement on the placement of the human. Now, do we discard all the good he has accomplished through the latter part of his existence or, do we take his entire lifespan as guidance? What is your answer, Azrael?"

"Am I to be party to the deeds, good and bad, or am I to make a choice purely on what you have said?"

The committee mumbles amongst themselves. Finally, they gave their reply.

"You are to make the decision on the facts that we have presented."

Azrael stared at the figures that sat before him, surely a man's ascension into the beyond could not be decided upon with so little to go on, could it?

"You disagree?" Boomed the voice.

"I merely beg your indulgence that you might offer me a fuller explanation."

"You do, do you? And what gives you the right to ask such a thing? No other Angel has asked for further explanation, why should you?"

He shifted again, this was becoming uncomfortable. No celestial questioned the committee and here he was, doing exactly that.

"I feel if the human has done one selfish act and one hundred selfless acts, that he surely deserves admittance into the great beyond. Humans make mistakes but are they not created in the Almighty's own image?"

Once again the mumbles went around the group.

"You may leave."

"You do not require my decision?"

"Not at this point. Leave now, we shall call you back when we have considered your argument."

Bowing he left the room, none the wiser as to the human they had referred to.

"How was it?" Dumah was waiting outside.

"Strange, very strange. They will call me back."

"No! What did you say? They have not asked for the others, or myself to go back."

"I did not say anything that a fair and reasonable Angel would not have said."

"You answered their questions?"

"No, I did not. I needed more information before I condemned another to damn nation."

"Oh, my. That will, as the humans say, put the cat amongst the pigeons. Why do you care so much for these selfish creatures? They fight, kill, lie and commit such abominable acts, yet you defend them still. Oh, Azrael my friend, they will be your undoing."

Dumah walked on, his head shaking from side to side as he tried to understand the Angels care for these Godless souls.

~

Brian entered the office, today he was to sign the document that would keep him comfortable for the rest of his life. The young solicitor stood as Brian came in.

"Good to see you Mr Felling, please have a seat. Help yourself to coffee and doughnuts. I have had the secretary draw up the paperwork and she will be in with it shortly. How was your weekend?"

Brian poured himself a coffee, maybe just one doughnut he thought as he placed it on the saucer.

"Very good thank you, how about you? Are you married, children?" Ridiculous questions he thought, the man looked barely out of college.

"It was good, thanks. Yes, I have a wife and 2 small children. We spent the weekend at her parent's beach house, so nice for the little ones to get away from the city now and then."

Brian gulped, the coffee seemed to go the wrong way. Jeez, he must be getting old! He imagined the man to be all of 22 or there about's. The solicitor continued.

"We were celebrating our 10th anniversary, really doesn't feel that long. You are no longer married I see from my notes?"

"That's right. We finalised the divorce last year. Congratulations on your anniversary, I have to say, I thought you were a lot younger than you obviously are."

The man laughed, his perfect white teeth glimmering in the sunlight.

"I have my mother to thank for that, people still mistake her for my sister if you can believe that and she's 63! A wonderful woman too." It was at this point that the secretary entered the room.

"I have your documents here, Mr Ramona, I'll leave them on the desk."

"Thank you."

Brian looked over the papers paying particular attention to the clauses that were brought to his attention by Mr Ramona, these consisted mostly of a no publicity agreement and a notification that he was not to speak to anyone concerning the settlement. Standard clauses in a case like this commented the solicitor. Happy with the terms Brian signed the documents.

"There will be a cooling-off period as is customary, if you don't change your mind in these days the funds will be transferred to the account you have specified. Now, with that in mind, we have various financial advisors that can talk you through options and investments. If this is something you will find useful we can set up some meetings in the coming months. That about sums up the business for now. Do you have any questions Mr Felling?"

Brian sipped his coffee, there was one thing he needed to ask, should he?

"Mr Felling? Anything you ask is in the strictest of confidence."

"My ex-wife, am I obliged to divulge this to my ex-wife?"

Mr Ramona laughed.

"Excuse my bluntness Mr Felling but you are not at liberty to tell your ex Jack shit. This is revenue received after your divorce, you have no offspring to support, therefore and in laymen's terms, you are free and clear."

Brian was visibly relieved, she had taken as much from him as he was going to allow.

The celebration was a low key one, mostly because they didn't want to draw attention to themselves. The table was booked at the restaurant with only Mel, Neil and Linda joining him. Brian said it was a celebration of his recovery, only he and Neil knew the real reason. Not even Linda was privy.

Brian had his first meeting with an accountant/financial advisor since he had given over the company. Mr Ramona had set it up with a firm that he knew to be reputable and discreet. Brian waited in the foyer of the large building, it was clear that the firm handled a lot of high-class clients by the décor alone. You didn't have these types of offices without hefty chunks of cash behind you. The receptionist called him over. Her perfectly manicured appearance left him feeling underdressed.

"If you would like to take the elevator to the 6th floor there will be somebody there to meet you."

"Thank you. 6th you say?"

"That's right Mr Felling."

The elevator played classical music, not the usual muzak that often filled the cramped space. This was class, the size of the elevator itself was twice as big as they normally were.

Brian was met at the doors by a woman that could have been the clone of the one that sat at the reception desk.

"If you would like to follow me, Mr Felling."

They walked down the airy corridor to the office at the glass-fronted end of the building. It all felt very grand to the man that only a few months ago could barely afford a cup of coffee.

He was shown into the plush room that looked more like a grand hotel suite rather than a financiers office.

"Do come in Mr Felling, would you prefer I call you Brian?"

"Brian is fine, it is my name after all." He laughed.

"Excellent. Right, I have spoken with Mr Ramona about your position and today is merely a fact-finding mission as to what you intend to do with such a vast and sudden accumulation of wealth. There are various options that we could take a look at if this is agreeable to you?"

The advisor took Brian through a mountain of options, so many that his head began to spin.

"Brian? Do any of these options sound like something you would be interested in?"

Brian rubbed his temples, he had never dealt with the money side of things in all the years he was married or ran a business. Maybe that was his undoing, maybe he should have taken more of a first-hand approach to these matters.

"Can I think it over?"

"Of course, you can, nobody expects you to make a decision straight away. It is a lot of money we are talking about, Brian. My job is to search out the best and most lucrative options for you and, should you decide to go with our firm, we are here to get you the best return. Make your cash work for you, so to speak. I have taken the liberty of emailing you some of the ventures we have discussed this morning, that you can go over them in your own time."

Brian shook his hand, picked up his jacket and left the imposing building with a brain full of numbers and names that he had no clue about.

Maybe he should talk with Neil, he was good with these kinds of things. Yes, he would call on his friend and get his thoughts.

9.

Rest Easy

Walking into the car showroom, he had come to the conclusion that he needed a new car. For the months since his divorce, he had been using a battered old Chevy that he picked up cheap. He didn't want anything too extravagant, no point drawing attention to his newfound wealth. Something reliable and comfortable would do just fine.

The salesman approached him, his ridiculous cowboy hat perched slightly askew on his head.

"Howdy partner, now don't tell me. I see you in one of our more luxurious vehicles, am I right? I can always tell a man with taste and you Sir, have that air about you. Am I right?"

Jeez, this one was a card. Brian had to fight back the urge to say, 'you're rooting' tooting' right partner.'

"Browsing my friend, just browsing. I'll give you a shout if I need assistance."

The salesman nodded, tipped his hat, and stood in the corner of the showroom as he watched the man carefully. There were 3 other salespeople in there and he didn't want to lose a commission to them.

After spending a good 20 minutes looking at the various cars on offer, Brian approached the man.

"Do you mind if I sit in that one? "He pointed to a shiny black pick-up truck.

"Be my guest, it's a particularly good example of its make. I can take you for a test drive if you have the time, give you a feel for its comfort and ease of use."

"That would be great, yes, a test drive would be better."

"I'll grab the keys, back in a minute."

An hour later, Brian was driving off the lot in the truck, it felt good to finally have a car that he didn't mind being seen in. He had loved his Jeep, unfortunately, Martha had made sure that he didn't get to keep it. This was better than the jeep in so many ways, it had all mod cons and the music system was ridiculously superb. This would do very nicely!

When he turned up at the coffee house he beeped the horn several times until eventually, she appeared at the door. Her smile radiated as the driver bobbed his head down to give her a wave.

"Fancy a ride in my new wheels?" He grinned.

Mel called back into the shop as she untied her apron.

"Cover me, back soon." The young man gave her a thumbs up, raising his head out of his phone. It had been a quiet morning, an even quieter lunchtime period.

"You sure you can get away?" Asked Brian as she climbed up to the seat beside him.

"No problem, I have a great relationship with the boss. Well, this is some set of wheels you have yourself here, I have to admit, she puts my old truck to shame."

"You think it's a, she? I was hoping to impress you with the manliness of the thing."

"Course it's she, her headlamps are feminine, whereas mine, well he's just a brute of a man." Their laughter could be heard as they drove off down the hot, dusty road.

~

Azrael was called back to the great hall. Upon entering he noticed that the committee was not the usual 6 or 7 but 1, that 1 being St Peter.

"Come forward."

He made his way to where the smaller figure sat.

"We have reached a decision, I wanted to discuss it with you as you were the only being to cause us to stop and think. We have looked over the human's life and, as you pointed out, the human had indeed accomplished many a great selfless act. We noted that he changed his path at an early age, never to do a selfish deed again. In light of this, we, the Elders, granted the human entrance into the great beyond."

Azrael was thrilled, he did not know the human and it certainly was not he that brought the human to the gates to be judged, still he was thrilled. In his soul it pained him whenever one was denied access, for having spent so many millenniums amongst them, he knew they were not all bad, some circumstances lead them astray. Some would say they were weak, they were human, that was the truth of it. Stepping forward he knelt before the Elder, his wings folding back on themselves.

"Thank you, your Holiness. I pray the decision will not be one you regret."

"Is there any other matter you wish to discuss, Azrael? Any more humans that you feel compelled to save?" St Peter eyed the Angel carefully as he spoke. Azrael could feel those eyes boring into him.

"No other matter."

"Very well, you may leave, but know this. I have been around since the beginning, I see more than I need to see, more than I want to see. Do not fail me Azrael, clean up your loose ends."

Dumah walked with Azrael through the meadow. The day was a warm, sunny one with a cooling breeze. They were headed for the house in the distance. It was a large house with off white weatherboarding that had not been painted for some time. The fence around the garden was falling down, rotting slats that had buckled under the weight of the elements of the passing years. Azrael opened the gate, the squeak was loud as it echoed through the still of the air.

"Do you remember when we came here last, Dumah?" He asked, pausing to hear the response.

"Yes, it seems only a small fraction of time, yet to these humans, it is a lifetime ago. I remember the child that sat on that very porch, what did she hold in her hand? I forget."

"She held the book of the Lord's words, she held it close to her chest. Do you think she was praying?"

Dumah shrugged, for he had only small memories of the child.

"I would like to think so. Do you?"

"She was, I could hear her amidst her cries. She prayed that her Grandfather was no longer in pain, that God would take him as an Angel. She prayed for nothing of herself, such a little one to have been left all alone in the world." He continued as they walked silently into the darkened room.

The elderly woman lay in the bed, a bed that had not seen clean linen in quite some time. Her gentle eyes flickered as though a light had been switched on.

"Who's there?"

The pair remained silent as they watched her frail body try to hoist itself further up the pillows. She did not look afraid as one would suspect of a human that thought a stranger was in their midst, instead, she smiled. Azrael smiled back, he realised that she could not possibly see him yet felt moved to all the same.

"I remember you." She continued. "You looked so bright, like the sunshine on a winter's day. Did Grandpa become an Angel? I often wondered, but who would I ask?"

"Can she see us?" Dumah was beginning to feel uncomfortable with the old woman's questions.

"No, Dumah, she cannot see us, she senses our presence as other's often do. Few can see us." Azrael made his way to the bed, he sat on the edge, no indentations could be seen in the mattress as they would be had a human sat there. He picked up the pale hand, staring at the puckered, loose skin with its brown patches of age. The hand was warm and soft, lifting his gaze she stared straight into his eyes.

"Will I see him when we go?" She asked quietly.

"You will. You have waited a long time, have you waited alone?" whispered Azrael. She nodded her expression one of sadness.

"I thought he would come back."

Azrael shook his head, such a wasted, lonely life spent waiting for a thing that could never be.

"She can see you!" Hissed Dumah. Azrael turned to his counterpart, his head shaking slightly from side to side.

"No, she senses her time, she cannot see me." The woman squeezed his hand as he spoke. He knew she could see him, hear him and that it served no purpose to relay this to Dumah.

"The time is close."

Azrael leant close to the old woman's face, he whispered into her ear, she smiled, a sigh escaped her lips as she whispered back. Taking her hand once more he helped her to her feet, they were back in the meadow. The sun shone down, the flowers smelt wonderful as the breeze picked up their scent.

"Thank you, it has been some time since I walked amongst the glory of nature. What a beautiful world we have, that he made all of this for us, don't you think?"

Azrael nodded, this earth was spectacular.

"Here." She leant and picked a small flower, tucking it into his gowns she patted the soft fabric with satisfaction. Dumah looked on in disbelief, that she put it in exactly the right place.

"You truly are a benevolent Angel." She whispered as the bright figure clapped his hands.

10.

Pastures New

~

Brian lay on his bed, he glanced at the notepad. He had been so busy the past few weeks that he had barely given it a second thought. He had meant to scan through it, purely out of curiosity when he thought he had recognised a name on the T.V. Now, what was that name? He rolled over and grabbed the now dog eared pad from the table. Flicking through the pages he stopped, pulled out his phone and opened up a browser. Typing the name into the search engine he gasped, he knew it! The name was of the man that had passed on in Montana. Lance Prendergast. He continued to type in more names from the pad, 2 came up as deceased, recently.

He lay back, what was he to do with this information? Should he do anything at all with it?

One thing was for sure, he really needed to talk about this with someone. But who? They would think him mad, not a position he needed right now with his bank balance being as hefty as it was. That would be the first thing to be taken from him, he couldn't risk that. No, he would have to make some enquiries quietly, on his own for now.

"What do you mean we're going to Italy? Why?" Brian laughed, his friends were so strange!

"I have just offered you an all-expenses-paid holiday in one of the most beautiful countries in the world and you're suspicious? Thank you was what I expected, not that it was needed, but no, you ask why. Really you guys, it's my treat for all of your support over the past months, please say you'll come." Linda grabbed him, her arms tight around his neck she jumped up and down in an excited frenzy.

"Honey, mind the wound. Does this mean you'll come?"

"Damn right it does, I don't know about Mr CSI over there but I'm in." She released her grip on Brian, her face a confused, somewhat surprised stare at her husband.

"Neil? They have fishing, haven't you been saying that you need a holiday?"

Neil shrugged, this was so out of the blue, he knew his friend had always been a generous man, generous to a fault, but wow! This was unreal, he didn't know what to say.

"It's a fantastic gift, Brian, we would never be able to repay this."

Brian shook his head, the disappointed look said everything to his friend.

"Oh, okay then. If it means that much to you. Where in Italy?"

"Does it freaking matter!" Screeched Linda as she threw her arms around her husband.

"I guess not." He laughed.

"Marasusa, if that means anything to you guys, it looks beautiful, never been myself. Do you think it would be too presumptuous to ask Mel? I doubt she gets much time off work, never met her boss but if I did I would have to question why he leaves her to run things."

Linda chuckled, Neil dug his elbow gently into her rib.

"What? Is it a secret?"

"Is what a secret?"

"She's her own boss stupid. Has the subject never come up? I can't believe you've been seeing her all this time and you don't know anything about her."

Brian was embarrassed, he actually knew very little about her and here he was, about to ask her to take a vacation halfway across the world with them. Pathetic! He berated himself. There was time to rectify the matter, he would spend the next week or so getting to know all he could about Mel, settled! The message he sent was simple and to the point.

Mel, I have realised that in all the times we have spent in each other's company, we spend that time discussing my life, my wants, my past, my likes/dislikes. This is no way to begin what I hope will be a long and happy friendship. Please come to dinner, tonight. The rules are these. We cannot talk about me. Copious amounts of bourbon and good food. See you around 7.30 x

Mel chuckled when she read the message, he was funny and so darn cute! Her reply was simple.

Agreed x

~

Azrael perched himself high on the top of the mountain, it was his favourite place for solitude, and that view! The Almighty had surpassed himself with this, this, well it could only be described as exquisite. His thoughts turned to the human, Felling. What was he to do about this man? The order of things was set out with very good reason, if it got out now, in a world already mixed and lacking in faith, there was no telling where it would end. He had to do something, but what? That was the dilemma he faced.

He was sure that Dumah would not keep it to himself for much longer. He worked well with the counterpart, however, even he was aware of the Angels longing to rise higher in the ranks. There are a few amongst us that have been less than charitable, he uttered to himself. Some had gone so far as to have been cast out in their efforts. Dumah would not hesitate to take his place, this he was certain of.

The clouds rolled around him now, breaking every now and again to reveal the tapestry that lay before his feet. His mind was made up, he would visit the Felling man again. It could well be that the human had other things that now occupied him, there was certainly a solid bond building between him and the female. All things considered, the man had escaped death, he should welcome that and get on with living the short span of life allocated to him.

~

Mel knocked at the door of the large townhouse, she stood back and admired its pristine appearance. It reminded her of the house she once shared with her late husband, she smiled up to the sky as a way of reaching out to him. They had enjoyed a happy time together while it lasted. Not the same as her new friend, it sounded like he had endured a rotten time, not to mention the deception that was uncovered toward the end. Mel was thankful that her union had been a trusting journey.

Brian came to the door, his pinny splattered with what could only be imagined as tomatoes. A-ha! If the woman had to hazard a guess at tonight's menu she would say pasta of some sort. Men liked cooking pasta, she imagined it was one of the simpler yet tastier meals a person could prepare, swish it up with a pre-made salad and a little garlic bread, followed by chocolate cake and you've got yourself a meal fit for a king.

"Hey, come in. I'm so glad you could join me. Now before you get too excited, it's only a pasta dish I've made. You eat pasta I take it? Oh, lord I should have checked! You do eat pasta?" Mel laughed, the poor man suddenly looked like a deer in the headlamps.

"Of course, I do, Brian. Who doesn't love pasta? Here, I brought wine, wasn't sure what you prefer so I got one of each." She passed the bag to her host as she slipped off her jacket.

"Through here?" She pointed as she walked down the hall to the lounge.

"That's it, go through. I'll be with you in a sec, red or white?"

"Red please, make it a large one it's been a day and a half."

Brian returned minus the apron. Toting a large glass of red wine in one hand, white in the other.

"Dig in. So, what has been so manic about your day? Rush on the Lattes?" He laughed as he sat beside her. He had given this some thought and after a quick call to Neil, they had decided this was the way to go.

"You don't want to put her in the friend zone buddy, sit right next to her." Had been his advice.

"No, nothing that exciting. That at least would send profits up. I had to go visit my mother, always a great experience. She lives outside of town, in a care home for the past 2 years due to her mind not being quite what it was." Mel stared out of the window, a wistful expression appearing to grace her face as she spoke.

"It must be very hard for you. Do you have other family?"

"My father passed away nearly 10 years ago now, she was never the same after that. They were as close as 2 people could be, it was nice to grow up with parents that adored each other. I have a brother, sister-in-law 2 nieces, a few cousins here and there. 1 Aunt that I haven't seen for a long time, that's about it. I imagine there are more, can't say I'm inclined to look them up, I always figured if they were around they would have come to Dad's funeral, they didn't."

Brian put his hand on hers, he felt he should do something. It was warm to the touch, she was a warm person throughout.

"What about you, Brian? What secrets do you hold?"

"Ah, we agreed that my mission is to find out all about you. I am not that interesting, to be honest, the little there is to know of me, well, you know it already. Tell me about your brother, is he local?"

"Not so you'd notice, truth is, I see more of my sister-in-law than I do of my brother. Strange really, we were so close as kids. My nieces are lovely, such little ladies they are. I suspect one of them to be more tom-boyish, mind you, she hides it well in her effort to keep up with her sister!" She chuckled to herself as she visualised the little girl constantly trying to keep her unruly curls in check whenever there was a family gathering.

"They sound great. Do you get roped in for sitter duties much?"

"Once in a while. When my husband passed away they were constantly calling me up to babysit, I think half of the time they sat around the corner in the car, merely a tactic to take my mind off other things."

Sitting back, his smile now faded. He didn't know her husband had died he assumed they had divorced. That told him how little he had asked the woman about herself and he was astounded at his lack of interest.

"I am so sorry, I never thought to ask. You must think I'm a terrible person."

Mel laughed, her nose wrinkled when she did, he had noticed this!

"Don't be silly, Brian. I didn't offer it up in conversation either so we are as bad as each other."

They drank the wine, Brian checking on the meal occasionally.

"Okay, dinner is served. If you would like to follow me to your table Madam."

He was funny! The table looked amazing, he had pulled out all the stops in his efforts to impress her. Napkins neatly folded as they would be in a top restaurant, cutlery in the right place, 2 glasses, one for water the other for wine.

"Wow! I am very impressed. You do this every night?"

"Good Lord no." He chuckled. "Unless you count putting the pizza from the box to the plate and I have to be honest, it doesn't always get that far."

The meal was, thankfully, a good one. He had managed to avoid burning or overcooking any of it. Yes, he thought, pasta was a good call. They chatted as they ate, Mel telling stories of her time spent with her nieces, Brian talking about the business he used to run. They talked for a while about Mel's husband, she smiled fondly as she told of their marriage and the things they would do together. They enjoyed camping weekends in the hills, dancing and he particularly loved karaoke. He was no Frank Sinatra, she said, but it made him happy.

"It sounds as though you had a wonderful marriage, I envy you that." And it was true, he envied anyone that could truly say they had been happy with their choice in a partner.

"We had our moments as most do, on the whole, we had an amazing friendship. Isn't that what it's all about?"

"It is. I am glad you have had a blessed life, Mel, I don't know you yet as well as I hope to but, I could not bear to imagine that you have suffered. I mean to say, I know you have suffered, you lost your best friend, oh my, I am getting this ass upwards aren't I?"

"I know what you mean, it's okay. Thankfully he didn't have a prolonged illness, if anything it was completely unexpected. Some think that's worse but I am just glad of the time we had and it was a time worth having."

She had such a way with words, logical thinking, that's what it was. She saw the good in every situation and that was rare these days. She leant over and kissed him on the cheek, taking him totally by surprise.

"What was that for?" He blushed.

"Oh, no reason, I felt like it."

"You are a kind woman, I can't remember when I've had such a pleasant evening home. Thanks for accepting my invitation Mel, it means a lot. Now, that chocolate cake isn't going to eat itself, is it?"

11.

Right Place, Right Time

~

Azrael watched the pair as they laughed and ate. He liked this female, he liked her the last time their paths had crossed. She had a serenity about her, he was sure that when her time came she would make the perfect celestial. That time would not be for a good long while yet, she had much to do before that day arrived. He felt that tingle, the one that reminded him he had work to do. One last look through the window at the couple, he sighed at a feeling held long ago that could never be again as he faded away into the night.

~

The rain was a welcome relief, it had been dusty and humid for some time now.

"Come on buddy, we need to get a move on if we're to get that flight." Called Brian to his friend. Linda and Mel sat in the back of the car, excited at the idea of getting away from it all for a few weeks at least.

"NEIL!! What are you doing in there, come on for heaven's sake." Cried Linda through the window. Neil came outside, patting his pockets as if checking he had not forgotten anything. He high fived Brian as he walked to the car.

"Hey, bud. You going to lock that or leave it open in case the neighbours need a cup of sugar?"

"Bloody hell, all that double-checking and I forget to lock the front door! Cheers pal."

Once settled in the car, Neil had everyone check their passports and documents, just to be sure he added.

"How do you 2 ever manage to leave the house?" Laughed Mel as she waved her passport in his face. Linda shrugged, she had come to terms with Neil's incessant checking over the years.

"Are we ready?" Called Brian.

"Aye, aye skipper."

"Then off we go."

The journey was a straightforward one, they arrived at the airport with a good hour to spare after check-in.

"I can't wait to get there, have you been to Italy Mel?"

"No, I hear it's beautiful. I would never have gone overseas on my own. Have you been?"

"God, no. The furthest we've managed is Alaska and even that was a work thing with Neil, cold as anything. Not my idea of a vacation."

The women chatted as they awaited their departure, Neil and Brian browsed in the kiosk at fishing magazines and car magazines. They paid hurriedly when their flight was eventually called. Brian had gone all out for the trip, he had spent many a time in cramped second class seating over the years, not today, he smiled to himself as he stretched his legs out.

"Jeez, Brian this is amazing! This must have set you back a tidy sum, buddy?"

"It's a tidy sum worth every cent, plus, I don't intend to make it a habit. I wanted to experience it once, I like it!" He laughed.

Linda sat in her seat, her face glowing.

"You gotta see the ladies, Mel. It's bigger than our bathroom at home, I kid you not."

Mel giggled, it felt so good to be amongst people that still had room in their minds to be in awe of something as simple as a bathroom.

Italy was, as expected, a beautiful place. Linda stood and stared at their surroundings as they stepped from the cab. It was breath-taking, she had never seen anything so old look so wonderful.

"Oh, would you look at it, Neil, look at it." Neil was looking, not a man that was given to outbreaks of sentimentality he was stunned.

"Bless, is that a tear in your eye?" His wife asked him quietly.

"Sun, the sun's brighter here don't you think." He hurriedly replied as he wiped the tell away.

"Not bad, eh? Shall we get rid of this stuff and explore or, does anyone need a lie down first?"

asked their benefactor with a note of accomplishment in his voice.

"Sleep is for wimps, I say let's see as much as we can while we have the chance." Offered Mel as she grabbed her bags and headed for the villa. The others followed suit and within minutes they were back on the road with map in hand, ready for the adventure to begin.

~

Azrael and Dumah had been exceptionally busy, as winter took hold in many parts of the world, so too did illness and death. It was a balance that had to be, for the humans it was random and heart-breaking, for the celestials it was a way of controlling the continuation of a species. There was always a reason, the Almighty had said as much. For some, they had completed their part in the grand scheme, for others, they were prevented from being a cog in a possible chain of events. It is a complicated yet necessary process they were told. Their role was not to question, simply to comply.

"Do you think they ever question why one should survive the un-survivable whilst another succumbs to a chance accident?" mused Dumah as they picked their way through the squalid streets of the slum area. They were looking for a boy, he was close, they could sense him.

"Humans question everything, even when they know the answer. It is their nature to be inquisitive. It is their nature to wonder why them, they can be selfish this we know for sure. They can also be selfless. They pray for the release of a loved one in pain, they offer up bargains, take me instead they pray. They do not know the reasonings to which we adhere."

"Seems like a lot of wasted time to me when they could be doing other things." Dumah was yet to see the purpose of his counterparts approach to humans that, in his mind, was a wasteful commodity on the earth.

"He's in here. It's a young one, tread carefully with your thoughts."

"He cannot hear me."

"He is young, he has not yet been corrupted, he will hear you and possibly see you. Be kind Dumah."

The child lay shivering on the bed, he was alone and he was dying. His eyes were red with coughing. Azrael approached gracefully, this was one of the hardest tasks he undertook in his role. It seemed unfair that one little human should play such a part thus having to be removed. It seemed unfair to him that the way in which the boy had lived was the only way he could be brought to this conclusion.

The boy had an age of 5, the parent had left a long time ago leaving him with an elderly guardian. The parent had many offspring, this one being one too many. They had to leave, for wheels had been set in motion. Should the boy continue to grow and the guardian pass over, the boy would be forced into a world that would turn his pure and innocent heart into one of a killer of men, one man, in particular, this could not be allowed for the man would come to do great things.

"Hello, are you cold?" Whispered Azrael as he pulled the thin cover over the child.

"Why must you talk to them?" Dumah hissed, his voice shrill.

"Would you like to come with me? It is warm and bright, you can play all day."

The child, too weak to answer, stared up into the brightness that spoke to him, his eyes telling Azrael what he needed to know.

"Sleep little one, when you awake you will feel better than you do now."

He whispered softly into the child's ear. The boy replied with barely audible words.

~

Brian and Mel sat on the bank of the Lake, it was an amazing view. A view that a person could watch all day if they had the time.

"Do you believe in God?"

Mel was startled by the question, it came from nowhere leaving her stuck for words for a few moments. Brian continued to stare at the Lake.

"That's an odd thing to ask. Yes, in answer to it, I do. Many question why I should after my husband passed so young, but still I believe. Do you?"

Brian gazed up at the clear blue sky, it was perfect here.

"I never thought I did, never really thought about it much at all if I'm honest. I've always held a faith, not sure in what exactly, just faith that there's something. Until recently, that is, since the accident."

Azrael's ears pricked up, along with the hairs on his spine. What was he doing? Surely he wouldn't?

"Go on." Encouraged Mel. She was curious as to what he was getting at.

"Now I do, I mean, I shouldn't be here, right? But I am, what to do with that is the question that keeps running around my mind. Surely that means something, that I have a purpose to do something good with my life, doesn't it?" He stared at Mel, waiting for an answer, hoping that she had one.

"I think, this is only my thoughts, that we have a purpose regardless of near-death experiences. If I have learned anything, it's that we aren't here forever."

"What if we could be?"

Azrael paced the floor. Don't be foolish, man!

"Don't be silly, Brian. Only in movies are there immortals. Have you been smoking some of Neil's herbs?" Her laughter rang through the air, echoing over the Lake and bouncing back along the mountains that surrounded them. Brian shook his head.

"Just a crazy thought, pay no attention to me. How are you enjoying the trip? Is there anywhere in particular that you want to visit?"

Azrael heaved a sigh of relief.

"Have you ever thought about travel, when you were married did you ever want to go anywhere? We talked about touring once, never got to do it mind you."

Brian laughed, only that morning did something spring into his mind about where he was.

"You might think this weird, wouldn't blame you if you did, this morning my phone reminded me that today would have been my 15th wedding anniversary. We always said that if the marriage lasted that long we would come to Italy. It wasn't the reason I came here, far from it, but strange how things pan out don't you think?"

Mel shook the blanket they had been sitting on, she folded it neatly as she processed what he had said.

"Maybe it was subconscious?"

"I don't know, it hasn't entered my head since the day we said it and even that was half-joking at the time. I haven't thought about it since, especially after everything that has happened."

"Do you think it was meant to be? Is that what you're saying? Is this why you asked the God question?"

"I'm not convinced it was meant to be, as I said, I never gave it a second thought afterwards, one of those things you say when you're young."

"Hmm, coincidence is a great thing isn't it?"

They climbed back into the rental car and headed back for the villa. They were going into the town tonight with Neil and Linda for a meal and possibly dancing, or so Neil had threatened. They were halfway there when they noticed a broken down car on the side of the road.

"Should we stop? It is very remote here, the poor thing could be waiting hours and it looks like she's alone." Mel suggested, she didn't like the idea of a woman stranded out here and the evening was drawing in.

Brian slowed the car down, wound down the window and thought about the little Italian he could remember.

"Hai bisog-no di aiuto? I not speak good Italian." he asked in the best broken Italian he could muster.

The woman tried to smile through her worried look.

"Thanking to you, I have a little English. I have broken the car down, I have to go to the Ospedale."

"Hospital?"

"Si, hospital. My papa, he is sick."

"Get in, we can take you to the hospital." Replied Mel. The woman locked her car and soon they turned around and were on their way to the hospital. The woman explained that she had a call to say her father had suffered a heart attack and she was to come quickly.

"It's no problem, we will be there soon." Added Brian putting his foot down harder on the accelerator.

12.

Solitary Moments

They arrived at the hospital where the woman thanked them endlessly.

"You are too very good, Grazie. My name is Natalia Catalano."

Brian knew that name, why did he know it? It was on his list, of course, it was. Not Natalia but Eduardo.

"Eduardo?" He spluttered.

"Si, Eduardo Catalano, you know? You come see, Si?"

Brian couldn't help himself, he had to see this man for reasons that he couldn't explain, nor wanted to.

"Mel, do you mind? I won't be too long."

Mel didn't mind, she was confused definitely but she didn't mind.

"Take as long as you need honey. I'll get a coffee."

~

Azrael was already in the room, Dumah standing close by.

"I told you we should have dealt with this sooner."

"Dumah, I understand your fears, I do, but this needs to be handled in a certain way which is in hand."

The woman rushed to the bedside, grasping the hand of her Father as she knelt beside him. Her speech was fast and intermittent with the sobbing of a bereft daughter. Brian stood back, almost in the corridor as he watched the pitiful sight unfold. Why am I here? Intruding on the last precious moments of a family that I don't even know. His mind was a whirl of self-jibing amid the bleeps of the machines that kept the old man clinging to life. Quietly he backed out of the room to the sound of the flat-line. He sat on the chair in the corridor, his hands propping up his face. What had he been thinking?

The tap on his shoulder brought him back to reality, the woman with her tear-stained face took his hand.

"Thank you, thank you for bringing me to say goodbye to my papa."

Mel hugged him when he walked into the small café, she could sense that something had happened in there.

"She said goodbye to her father, it was very sad to watch."

"You did a good thing by taking her. You see, maybe you were meant to be here after all." She said quietly.

"Funny thing is, Martha would never have allowed me to pick up a stranger, not a charitable woman."

The drive back was quiet, they listened to music in a strange language, neither of them minding too much.

"Oh my God! Look, look at that." Cried out Mel as they neared the place they had rescued the woman. A lorry had all but smashed the small car to pieces, what remained of it was strewn all over their path.

"Jeez, this day keeps on giving. I hope nobody is hurt. Can you see a sign of anyone on your side?"

Mel strained her eyes to see down the embankment, spotting a man in overalls she pointed.

"There, down there."

Brian raced down to where the man sat, he looked dazed.

"Mel, call for help. My phone is in the glove compartment, the satnav should give you our location."

"Bloody hell you have had a day of it." Neil couldn't believe what he was hearing from his friend.

"We can stay in tonight if you'd rather not go out, wouldn't blame you its been one hell of a day out for you guys." Suggested Linda as she poured them a stiff drink.

"No, that's not fair on you 2, you were looking forward to it, plus I think it would do us good." Replied Brian as he sank the drink in one.

~

Azrael smiled at Dumah, he never gloated, that was not the way of celestials.

"Okay, I give you that one. It had to be him and it had to be today." Mumbled Dumah as they glided through the hospital corridors.

"Chain of events, Dumah, they have to be so."

They watched a while as Dr Natalia Catalano pulled on her scrubs and headed for the theatre. Her patient was prepped and ready to receive her transplant, it would be a success, this was a certainty.

The Doctor looked tired after the day's events, she would cope, it was her job.

The meal was fantastic, they all ate far too much, drank more than enough, and finished off the night dancing in the local nightclub. The nightclub was mostly holidaymakers from the States,

Germany, and the EU. Neil was happy that he didn't have to keep referring to the small book to translate every sentence. He loved the Italian language and the accent but he did find it hard work. Linda had picked up a few useful words in the couple of days that they had been there, mostly grocery item essentials it was fair to say.

They slept well that night, waking when the sunlight flooded their rooms. Cries rang out from the rooms as the evening drinking caught up with the occupants of the villa.

"My head is going to explode! What was I drinking last night? Why did you let me drink so much, you're supposed to protect me. Wasn't that in our wedding vows?" Neil staggered to the kitchen, feeling for the warmth of the coffee pot he filled the cup to the brim.

"I'm your wife, not your nanny. I don't remember vowing to be your mother, and can you not shout so loud?" Linda had her sunglasses on, the sun was far too bright for her head to deal with today.

"Does anybody else feel that we're getting too old for nightclubs, or is it just me?" Mel asked as she made her way slowly to the patio ser on the balcony.

"Amen to that sister. Never again, that's what I say, this time I mean it. Neil, our days of clubbing are over, you hear me?"

Only Brian seemed unaffected by the colossal amount of alcohol they had consumed. He had made coffee, started on the breakfast of bacon, egg and tomatoes for those that wanted it. In fact, he whistled away happily as the trio filled their systems with caffeine.

"You never get a hangover buddy, how do you do that? As far back as I can remember you have never suffered the dreaded effects of a damn good night. How? Tell me your secret." Brian laughed as he watched his friend in all his unsightly torment.

"Luck, I guess. That and I don't mix my beer, much. You were drinking everything on the bar list, no wonder you feel rough."

"Rough! I don't feel rough, I feel like I'm dying here."

"Mel, did you sleep okay? How's your head?"

"Shh, I am suffering. No sudden noises until the coffee has done its thing."

"Pathetic, that's what you are. You're grown-ass adults that should be used to drinking. I feel let down."

"You mock my friend, we are rebels of our time."

"You are marshmallows, my boy, gooey on the inside and not able to hack it anymore." Brian chuckled as he placed the steaming breakfast plates before the sorry looking trio.

"Plans for the day, Anyone?"

Linda groaned, all this perkiness was hurting her head more than it did already. Throwing the warm roll at her friend she shook her head carefully.

"Plan for today is this, I plan to get to know my friend bed a little better. Not sure what you all had in mind but that's what I'll be doing."

"Noo! Linda, we have so much to see. Your head will feel better for a bit of fresh air, not cooped up in here all day. Tell her Neil, you know I'm right."

Neil shook his head, he knew better than to disagree with his wife.

"Sorry buddy, you're on your own with this one."

"Mel, are you going to stay here too?" Brian could sense he was fighting a losing battle.

"Afraid so Brian, you get yourself out and explore, we'll manage. Somehow." Her smile, even when she looked as hungover as the others she still managed that enchanting smile.

Brian took the car, they were too far out to walk anywhere and the others had no intentions of venturing out this morning, at any rate. He drove down to the village, it was a quaint olde world village. The type of place that time had forgotten. He loved it. After parking the car he walked slowly around the centre square, it had a fountain that splayed pretty water displays into the air from the trumpets of Angel cherubs. He thought about his experience, or was it a dream? Either way, his mind took him to that place. The sound of those voices still rattled around in his head. Sitting on a bench he watched as 2 young children ran in and between the water jets, so innocent in their play as they splashed water at each other.

"You are on holiday?" Came the voice from behind him.

"Yes, are you?"

"No, I live here, my family has lived here for generations. It is a beautiful town, don't you agree?"

"I do. You speak very good English."

"I studied in England for many years, this place pulls you back. I hope you enjoy your time here. Try the café on the corner, it has delicious food, there is also the church on the hill if you are stuck for something to do."

"Thank you, I will." Brian turned expecting to see a person standing there, much to his surprise there wasn't. Turning back to the fountain in confusion he realised that the children had gone.

"Well, that wasn't strange much!" He said aloud in the empty square.

"Where have you been? We thought you would be back ages ago. Have you eaten?" Mel asked as Brian strolled through the garden that surrounded the Villa.

"I took a walk in the town, turned into quite a long walk by the end of it. You have to come with me, it's so amazing. I found the church, which must have been built hundreds of years ago but God it's beautiful. I spoke to a few of the locals too, can you imagine living in a place with so much history?"

"I'd be happy to go with you. Did you eat? We had a light lunch, Neil and Linda are feeling much better now, me too. A day off did us the world of good."

"I did, thanks. I had pizza as recommended to me by a person." Mel laughed.

"A person? Not a man, or woman?"

"Yeah, it was a strange conversation. They were standing behind me but when I turned they'd vanished. Mind you, it's a small courtyard type of centre so they probably wandered off."

Neil appeared on the balcony, his arms waving to the friend below.

"Hey buddy, you've been gone a long time. We were thinking of heading off for a stroll, I saw in the booklet they have a decent walking trail. Care to tag along?"

"Give me 2 secs to change my shoes and I'm there. Mel? You fancy a walk?"

Mel lifted the sunglasses to perch on top of her head, she had spent the day reading a novel of sorts.

"Yes, sounds good to me. This." She waved the book toward him. "Started off funny, now I feel like I want to throw myself into the sea on the heroine's behalf!"

Brian chuckled, he had read a similar book recently, they pull you in with the promise of a light-hearted read then wham! It's all doom and despair.

"Come on then girl, get your boots on and we should catch the sunset."

~

The trail was a well picked out trek through some incredible scenery, topped only by the orange sky as the sun began its descent over the hills.

Azrael sat atop his favourite resting place as he did often. He watched the 4 humans with interest as they made their way along the winding paths. He saw Brian gently take the hand of the female. The lights bounced magnificently through her hair, changing it from gold to red to orange. He wondered what the human touch felt like, for as an Angel he had never been permitted to have relations with another, their work was far too important to have anything distract them.

Had he been human he imagined he would have had many children, he was captivated by their laughter, their innocence in all things. Yes, he would have had at least 5 if not more. He sighed, it wasn't a thing he missed for he had never experienced it. Once, he would like to have been that man who held the hand of a delicate creature as the man he was following did now.

Dumah appeared beside him.

"Anything to report?"

"No, they are enjoying the bounty of nature. Look Dumah, have you ever seen such a wonderous sight?"

Dumah stared blankly at the sky, he was not a sentimental being.

"It is simply the sun setting Azrael, it does so every night as sure as it rises every morning, it shall continue to do so for a long time to come. I see nothing more than a repetitive function."

Azrael shook his head, how could he not see what he saw?

"I think it's a miracle, one of the Almighty's finest works. See, how the colours change so quickly and yet they still blend together perfectly." He knew his words were falling on ears that did not value the intricacies of art.

"Hmm, as you wish. I came to tell you we are needed, there has been a rockslide on the other side of the earth, many to be taken this night. It was a difficult one to set, but the job is now done. Come."

~

Brian loved Italy, now that he had done what he came here to do he was free to enjoy the rest of their time in the beautiful country. Part of him wished he could stay here, that wasn't an option and he told himself that millions of people who go on holiday say the same thing wherever they go, still, if he could pick up tomorrow and set himself up with a nice little villa. Nothing too flashy, a simple home coupled with a simple lifestyle, he would be happy.

"Hey, Brian?" It was Mel, she knocked at his open door.

"In here, come in." Mel stood at the bathroom door watching as Brian pulled on his sneakers.

"What's all this? Is it a work thing?" In her hands, she held the notepad with all the scraps of paper he had used for jotting things down when he was out and about.

"Not exactly, it's a little project that I've been working on. It's nothing really, silly scribblings that I ought to throw away. Are they ready to go?"

"Yes, we thought we'd leave in around 30 minutes if that works for you. Is this the name of that poor old guy who's daughter we picked up?" Mel's puzzled expression as she scanned through the pages told Brian that she did not find these scribblings silly, more worrying judging by the changing look on her face.

"They're nothing, honestly, that name was a fluke. I mean, there are thousands of people in this region with that name. Imagine it as the equivalent to Smith or even Chan."

Mel nodded as she handed the pad back to its owner.

"Not my business, I'm sorry if it appears I was snooping. Right, come on, we have a boat to catch." She hurriedly left the room leaving Brian sitting in the chair dismayed.

13.

Gone Fishing

They were going on a fishing trip, the guys had been looking forward to this day since they had arrived. Neil was a keen fisherman when time off allowed him. Brian only occasionally, still, it was what promised to be a relaxing day on the lake. They had a cooler full of food and another containing cans of beer. Perfect!

Their guide for the day was an older man, highly recommended by the owners of the villa. He spoke some English, enough to get a conversation going along with instructions regarding safety on the small boat.

"Mel, have you fished before?"

"I can't say I have, Neil, It always seems a relaxed sport, I'm looking forward to giving it a whirl. How about you Linda, do you go with Neil?"

"Lord no, that's Neils quiet time where he can get away from me and the kids for a few hours. I'm honoured that he invited me along today. It's the bait you see, I never could get on with all that worm hooking, seems cruel to me."

"They can't feel it, honey." Her husband laughed.

"You don't know that Neil, you tell yourself that to make yourself feel better."

"Should be a nice day all the same. You ladies can have a go or sit in the sun, yapping."

"We're not puppies, you wiener!" retorted Linda, slapping his behind as he passed her.

"You okay there buddy? You're quiet today."

Brian nodded, he felt a little out of sorts. He was sensing a cooler vibe from Mel and could not for the life of him figure out why.

"All good over here Pal."

They sailed a fair distance before the older man found a good starting point. He quickly explained what they could catch, what they should throw back and what to do in the event that a person fell overboard. All standard instruction to Neil.

"Why do they throw some back?" It was Mel that quietly asked the question.

"The young, we don't take the young. We take what we need and no more."

"Ah, I see." Made sense, she thought.

Linda stretched out on the chair, carefully covering her skin with sun cream as she watched her husband cast his first line into the blue water.

Mel held the reel in her hands, she felt easier that she had been attached to a harness, the risk of being dragged into the deep lake by a shark was not one she was willing to take no matter how much her brain told her there were no sharks in the water. Gazing across the vast lake she smiled to herself, what a beautiful place they had chosen and such a glorious day. Her eyes paused as she took in the figure of the man that she thought she was beginning to know quite well, was she? The incident with the names was more than a coincidence, she was astute enough to know that much.

Brian looked across at her now, her stare intense. What was she thinking, what had he done that had caused her to have that look of mistrust? She averted her eyes back to the water below. They were both distracted from their thoughts by the screeching of an excited Neil as his reel began to spin, almost out of his control. He had hooked something and it was a large something. With the expert help of the older guide, they guided the fish closer to the boat, it was heavy, Neil had to work hard to reel in the creature that tried to get away.

"What is it?" called Linda from her sunbed.

"Not sure, hon, I'll let you know when we get the monster on deck." Neil's voice was breathless as he shouted back to his mostly uninterested wife.

"Zander, he a big one. Make for you a tasty meal." Smiled the guide. It pleased him that they caught something on their trip. Good advertising for the small business he had built over the years. Leaning carefully over the side, net in hand, the fish had no option but to swim into it. Heaving the heavy net up and bringing the fighting fish to its resting place on the deck he stood back to look at it.

"Big! Very big. We take a photo, Yes?" unhooking the monster carefully he felt proud.

~

Azrael never understood this human sport. Shaking his head from the mountain view he watched the whole activity of the capture, the human holding it high as a trophy followed by the picture-taking with a camera. He knew that these processes had been a necessary process for many over the years as a means of sustenance, however, he never could get on board with doing it just for the fun of it. They were a curious being in that some valued their own lives to the utmost and yet, they thought nothing of ending another's, be it animal or human.

It had been a difficult week, as weeks go, for the Archangel. He had been called back to speak with the committee several times, he had the feeling they knew something, he was not about to offer himself up until he had exhausted all options.

Dumah, he felt, would not be as generous if he were to be pressed.

Time to get back to work, his wings spread gracefully, their bright whiteness mixing with the camouflage of the clouds around the peak of the mountain he stood upon.

Brian stared at the spot high up in the distance, he could have sworn he saw a swan take off from the mountain top. A large swan too! The boat began its return to shore, a good day of fishing had been accomplished with all 3 catching something. They thanked their guide as they left the jetty. Neil held the cooler bag carefully as he made his way to the car.

"Are you going to cook it?" asked Linda.

"Are you crazy woman? There's a place in town where they will prepare and cook what you catch, the fella said his son owns it and it's part of the package. Not a bad deal, eh?"

"Do we need to go back to change?" asked Mel.

"You look lovely as you are, besides, I think it's pretty casual from what the guide was saying. Neil, we don't need to change for this place do we?"

"No bud, go as you are the old fella said."

Arriving in the town Brian caught Mel's arm before she went into the small restaurant.

"Have I upset you, Mel? You seem a bit quiet with me today."

Mel gently pulled her arm away, she felt confused, she wondered if this was her making something of nothing as a way of distancing herself from any emotional attachment to the man.

"I'm okay, Brian. Bit of a headache if I'm honest, nothing personal."

Well, that was a relief. Brian was happy with the explanation, why he worried so much was beyond him. Women get funny when they have headaches. Sorted! Mel liked the fact that men were oblivious to the ways of a woman's mind.

The fish was prepared and served to the waiting customers. There was plenty left that they could take with them, the waiter had informed them although Neil was happy for them to use it up themselves. It was nice to have, here in this place but he didn't fancy being the one to have the villa stink of fish for the rest of their stay. The waiter was thrilled, having had a few more customers ask for the dish the foursome were busy tucking into it made the chefs afternoon a little less arduous.

~

As with all things heavenly, Azrael had various tasks that were pleasant. One such task was the welcoming of new life into the world. Not that he interfered much with this side of things, more an overseeing role. This one was running later than expected, he hovered around in the background as the familiar sound of cries rang out through the dwelling. He watched in wonderment as the humans cried their thanks and gratitude for a successful arrival.

They were sweet little things, these human babies, all pink and soft as yet unaffected by worldly traits. He loved the innocence of it all. Of course, he knew what lay in store for them, that went without saying, still it was these first moments that tugged at him. The promise of what could be. Dumah, ever close by, could not see what the fuss was about. In his thoughts, he saw them as just another in the long line of humans that would grow to become the greedy and selfish beings that he saw them to be.

"Well, that's another one safely delivered. Do you never tire of it? You watch them as though it is the first time you have seen one appear in this world."

"But it is, it's the first time that particular human has smelt the fragrance of their surroundings, breathed their first breath, felt their first touch. Can you imagine what that must be like? Do you never wonder?" Azrael asked of his counterpart.

"No, I never wonder. I simply ask myself what foolishness will this one bestow upon the world."

Azrael shook his head, he pitied this Angel. They were given these tasks, not only as overseers but to learn. It would appear Dumah had learnt nothing in the centuries at his side.

"This position is not always the right one for some."

Dumah shrugged, he could think of better positions an Angel such as he might take to, until then he would serve his time dutifully. He had leverage, he intended to eventually use it well.

The holiday was coming to its end, they had all enjoyed their time in the beautiful villa, alas it was now time to pack up and head home. Neil had spent a lot of his days taking photographs, it was a hobby he had neglected over the past years, a shame as they were extremely good. He had the eye, as Linda called it. The couple had gotten closer without the daily checklist and teenagers to contend with. Brian had noticed this, it was good to see the couple as they were when he first knew them. Mel had gotten over her headache quickly, she and Brian had returned to the comfort of their budding friendship. Yes, it had been a welcome break for all.

The rental car loaded, they said a last farewell to the villa reaching the airport in good time. It wasn't until they were taking out the suitcases that Brian realised he had left his notepad on the bedside table, it came to him in a flash.

Dumah held his breath, what will he do? Make a decision human. Azrael felt sad, it had to be done, there was no other way.

"Damn it, I have to go back. I left something."

"No, you're kidding aren't you?"

"No joke buddy, we've got plenty of time. I'll take the car and be back before you know it. The plane doesn't leave for another 2 hours."

"Can't you get the owners to forward it? Unless it's your passport of course and then, Yeah, you best go get it. Is it your passport?" asked Mel quizzically.

"Yeah, yeah it's my passport. Stay here, get some lunch on me and I'll be as quick as I can. If there's any problem I will get the next flight and see you back home."

Kissing Mel on her lips he felt a flicker of electricity run through him.

"Drive carefully." They called after their friend as he disappeared down the road.

~

"You can see now that he is not going to leave it alone?"

"Yes. I had hoped, no matter. This past week I have moved various things to accommodate the gap. What should be will still be."

For the first time, Dumah could feel the pain of his counterpart, he did not enjoy it as he assumed he would. Stretching his arm he placed it around the Archangels shoulder.

"Would you like me to do it?"

"That is kind, no, I have to do this."

~

Brian almost hit the wall when the large being appeared in the seat beside him. Jeez, he was hallucinating again. It must be aftereffects of that blasted accident, when would they stop? As soon as he got home he would make it his priority to speak with the doctor about this.

"Don't be scared, Brian. You remember me?"

"Christ, now I'm hearing things."

"You are hearing what you need to hear. We asked you, implored you to leave well enough alone. Do you recall?"

Brian could, this was no hallucination, they were back and they were very real.

"Okay, okay I get it. I'll turn the car around, forget I ever saw you, forget I ever saw the damn list. Give me another chance, please."

Azrael shook his head solemnly, he knew the man meant what he said, for now. Sadly, he knew that this human would keep coming back to the thing that could not be meddled with.

"I am going to give you a choice. You are human after all, your life is a series of choices whether you realise it or not. Go left, go right, simple yes? But never stand still, that's how it works. Ultimately you have 2 paths, this makes it easier for us to predetermine fate, without it, well… It is not your concern. What is your concern right now is this choice. You, or your flight? Many people, some you are fond of or you? What do you choose?"

Brian was scared, it all sounded so final to him. He had just gotten his life back on track and was happy. Why was he such a bull-headed idiot! Why did this thing obsess him so much?

"Can't you wipe the memory? You are Angels, right? You must have powers, if you can determine who stays and who goes then surely you can wipe a memory? I didn't even want to know all of this, it keeps me up nights, I don't know why or what it all means, all I know is if I hadn't seen it, surely you can understand that? You're things of God, God is good isn't he?" The man was panicking, Azrael was absolute in what he had to do.

"I'm sorry, it has to be this way."

Dumah was shocked, he expected Azrael to be swayed by the human's pleading. He sat in the back of the rental, his mouth open yet no words leaving his lips. He watched as the man shook, his hands barely able to keep the steering wheel steady.

"Brian?" Azrael's voice echoed throughout the car as it careered along the bends on the beautiful hillside.

"Brian, have you chosen?"

"Azrae…"

"Please, Dumah be silent. You asked me to deal with the matter, I am dealing with the matter."

"We can do what he asked, we can lose the memory. It is not unheard of, I think he has learnt the lesson we wanted him to learn. Azrael, think about what you are doing, I beg you."

14.

There is Always a Plan

The alarm clock rang, rolling over Brian hit the snooze button. He looked at the woman lying next to him, man, he was a lucky son-of-a-bitch. He stroked the soft hair that lay tangled over her face. It was as soft as the first time he had stroked it nearly 20 years ago, she had a few more fine lines on her face than she had then, but she was still his beautiful Mel. Her eyes opened.

"What you staring at fella?" She smiled as she spoke softly.

"Oh nothing, just the most beautiful wife a man could hope for."

"You're so soppy." She laughed as she wrapped her arms around his neck.

"What's the plan for today?"

Mel kept hold of her husband as she rolled her eyes up to the ceiling and thought. Jumping up in the bed she looked across at the clock.

"We have the meeting at the community centre, remember? I'm so excited! Are you?"

"I am, it feels good to give back. I always felt a bit of a cheat when I got so much cash after the accident, feels good that we have put it to good use."

The meeting went as they hoped it would. The mayor stood at the podium, his round face red with pride as he began his speech.

"Welcome all, to this special occasion. Stand up Mr Felling, Mrs Felling. Give a warm applause to our wonderful benefactors for this, the opening of their 8th homeless shelter. Not only will it provide the unfortunate with a place to hang their hat, but it will also, as the other centres do, provide these young people with a place of learning. Now, to cut the ribbon, we are delighted to hand over to one of the first young men to have used this lifeline in the flagship centre, Benjamin Hampson. Get up here Benjamin."

The audience clapped and cheered as the man, of around 35 stepped up to the podium.

"To say this saved my life, well it seems too small a phrase. As many of you have read, I was a runaway, in trouble with the law and quite frankly headed nowhere fast. Brian and Mel took a huge risk with me, I'm happy to say that risk paid off. They put me through college where I found my interest in medicine and science. From there I joined a pharmaceutical company, worked my butt off, I might add, and 5 years ago was in charge of the department that lead the way in new treatments for cancer. All of this, I owe to you guys. All of our patients that have had their lives changed, they owe their lives to you." With teary eyes, he cut the ribbon.

~

Azrael sat in the seat beside the rest of the committee, their purpose here today was to introduce Dumah to his new counterpart. He beamed with pride as the Angels stood before them. He had been on the committee for a while now. Dumah had no idea that the human was his test, Azrael had great faith that he would do the right thing and he was proved right.

"Come forward. Do you know why we have called you here this day?" Boomed the familiar voice of the middle seat.

Dumah stepped forward, Azrael thought his features seemed softer now, less taut.

"I do."

"Excellent. This is Raguel, Raguel, this is Dumah. Work well and in harmony. Go with the blessing of the Almighty."

Dumah waited for Azrael to finish his other business.

"Old friend, it has been too long. How are you faring up here, do you miss our time together?"

Azrael smiled, he had missed the Angel in his own way.

"You are pleased with my replacement?"

"That remains to be seen. I came here to beg a favour if you would be so kind." Dumah crooked his finger, Azrael followed.

They stood quietly at the back of the crowded room, listening to the man speak. The woman held his hand tight, her face glowing.

"I often wondered why this one, now I see. I look back on the time and see how it all had to be so, the chinks in the armour as the humans say. I have watched this one carefully, so many that he has saved, so much those he has saved have done for the betterment of their kind. Did you always know?"

Azrael watched the face he had come to feel a fondness for, there were few like this one.

"I was part of that lesson?"

"I hoped, Dumah. I always hoped."

As Brian walked to the back of the room he felt a rush of warm air that enveloped him in the strangest of feelings, it was a feeling of great comfort felt only when a mother hugs a child. A familiar feeling, that told you everything was as it should be and would be just fine.

Printed in Great Britain
by Amazon